To my dismay, Ryan filed in behind me. "Pretty weird that we're on the same trip, huh?" he said, tapping me on the shoulder.

"Yeah," I said, "small world."

"And I bet you're just so glad to see me," he said in a sarcastic tone as I stepped up to the sink.

I rolled my eyes. "Oh? Why do you think that?"

"Because now you'll have a guy to set up your tent and protect you out in the wilderness," he teased. "I'm not just brains, you know. I'm quite an outdoorsman—I can help you with anything you can't do."

"Please," I responded, annoyance creeping up my spine.

"What's the matter, Brennan?" Ryan went on. "Afraid that I might outdo you in the athletic department too?"

My hands tightened with anger around my water bottle. Then I was struck by a brilliant idea. I stepped to the right, placed my fingers directly on the faucet head, and "accidentally" sprayed Ryan with water.

"Hey!" Ryan yelped in surprise.

"Oops," I said innocently. "Didn't mean to getcha."

Love Stories

Falling for Ryan

Julie Taylor

BANTAM BOOKS
NEW YORK · TORONTO · LONDON · SYDNEY · AUCKLAND

RL 6, age 12 and up

FALLING FOR RYAN

A Bantam Book / September 1998

Produced by 17th Street Productions, a division of Daniel Weiss Associates, Inc.
33 West 17th Street
New York, NY 10011.
Cover photography by Michael Segal.

ISBN: 0-553-49252-7

Published simultaneously in the United States and Canada

Bantam Books are published by Bantam Books, a division of Bantam
Doubleday Dell Publishing Group, Inc. Its trademark, consisting of the
words "Bantam Books" and the portrayal of a rooster, is Registered in
U.S. Patent and Trademark Office and in other countries. Marca
Registrada. Bantam Books, 1540 Broadway, New York, New York 10036.

PRINTED IN THE UNITED STATES OF AMERICA

OPM   0 9 8 7 6 5 4 3 2 1

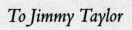

To Jimmy Taylor

One

"I CAN'T BELIEVE I lost the election," I moaned for what must have been the hundredth time. Letting out a deep breath, I tried to regain composure and stared at my teary-eyed, blotchy-faced reflection in the school bathroom mirror.

"I know," said my best friend, Jenni. She handed me a tissue from her overflowing backpack. "It's completely lame that Ryan Baron beat you by fifty lousy votes. I mean, *please*."

Ryan Baron. Ryan Baron. Ryan Baron. The name repeated itself in torturous circles around my brain.

Suddenly tears crowded my eyes all over again. "Ugh! Why did you have to mention his name?" I blurted out in frustration, ripping the tissue Jenni had handed me into little pieces.

"Wow, Kylie, I'm sorry. But really, try to chill for a sec and . . . ," Jenni began.

I could barely register her words. My mind was

too busy reeling with flashes of Ryan Baron and his know-it-all smirk. My pulse accelerating, I remembered the time in seventh grade when he sabotaged my science project so he could beat me in the science fair, the time he cross-examined my oral report on the War of the Roses freshman year so that he could show how much he knew and make me look stupid, the countless times this past year that he'd yelled out the answers in precalculus so that he could get them out before I could, the time—"Ugh! I'm so angry!" I yelled, kicking the base of the sink with my platform sandal. That wasn't the smartest move. "Ow!" I screamed. I bent down to massage my throbbing toe.

Jenni squatted to meet me eye level. "Kylie."

"Yes?" I responded in a shaky voice.

Concern clouded her large brown eyes. "You *must* chill out."

I stood up slowly, letting out another deep breath. Poor Jenni. I *was* acting like a maniac. At least there was no one else around to witness my breakdown— school had ended about twenty minutes ago. I looked down at my feet, concentrating on my now swollen big toe. "I'm sorry."

"It's all right," Jenni said, handing me some more tissues. "It's just that I've never seen you like this before. Take a minute and try to calm down," she suggested, leading me over to the small bench by the window.

I dropped down next to her, sighing heavily. She was right—I needed to collect myself. I played with the crumpled tissues in my hands. "I know I'm overreacting, Jen," I said. "He just makes me so mad! I mean, the only reason he won is because he promised stuff like Fiona Apple playing at our prom next year."

Jenni smiled slightly. "Yeah. As if an alternative megastar is dying to come to Oklahoma City to perform for free in a high-school cafeteria. I don't think so."

"Right?" I said, suddenly laughing at the absurdity of it all. "Ryan's never going to be able to deliver all the stuff he promised. Bands in the cafeteria on Fridays, an excused absence on your birthday, abolishment of the no-designer-logo dress code. What does he think this is, *Beverly Hills, 90210*?"

"See?" Jenni squeezed my hand. "There's no way Ryan can push through the ridiculous things he promised. He'll be the worst student body president in the history of Jefferson Memorial. Probably in the history of Oklahoma City. *That's* your payback."

"Yeah," I said, leaning my head against the wall and closing my eyes. "But now I'll never get to start the programs *I* proposed—the free SAT prep courses, the plant-a-tree program, the date rape awareness seminars. Those were things that would've made a difference. Now they'll never happen."

Jenni patted my arm consolingly. "We can still try to do some of that stuff on our own—round up

3

people to plant trees after school, that type of thing. Your dreams don't have to die just because you lost."

Jenni's words echoed in my head. *You lost.* Not only had I lost, but I'd lost to Ryan Baron. "It just makes it so much worse that he's in just about every one of my classes."

"Well, that's your own fault for being so darn smart and being in all honors," Jenni teased.

"Seriously, Jen." I rubbed my eyes dry. "I have to see his stupid, cocky smile, like, twenty-four seven."

"At least the year's almost over," Jenni pointed out. "And that trip of yours is just around the corner."

I sighed. "Just three more weeks. It's the only thing that's keeping me going." I smiled despite myself, thinking about how ecstatic I'd been the day I'd brought the Adventure Trails poster home from school and my parents had agreed to send me on the trip. "Eighteen days of roughing it in the great outdoors. I can't wait." I stood up, straightening out my short purple skirt. "No problems. No school. No Ryan."

"Atta girl!" Jenni jumped up beside me and put her arm around my shoulders. "You're going to have a killer summer. You have so much to look forward to."

"You're totally right," I said, feeling somewhat rejuvenated. I stepped up to the mirror. I didn't look *that* bad. My fair skin wasn't too blotchy anymore, and my shoulder-length blond hair looked pretty much in order. "And I'm not going to let Ryan get to me. Pretty soon I'll be hundreds of miles away from him." I pulled out some lip gloss and began to apply it to my lips. "Maybe I'll even drop honors next year so that I don't have to ever see his idiotic face again." I smiled.

Jenni laughed. "That might be taking it a little far, but I'm glad to see the old Kylie is back."

I turned and gave Jenni a tight hug. "Thanks for putting up with me," I told her.

"Please, don't even mention it." Jenni shook her head, and her dark curls bounced over her shoulders. She grabbed her backpack up off the floor. "Tell you what. Why don't we get out of here and go drown our sorrows at Tastee-Freez?"

"Double chocolate marshmallow sundaes?" I asked enthusiastically, lifting up my own bag and squaring it on my shoulders.

"But of course." She linked her arm in mine. "I wouldn't have it any other way."

Feeling a renewed sense of happiness and confidence, I pushed open the bathroom door and Jenni and I walked down the hall, our platform heels clicking against the linoleum.

You're going to be fine, I told myself as we strolled along the gray-painted lockers. *Who cares about Ryan Baron anyway? You can't let him get to you when you have so much to look forward to.*

But my resolution was instantly forgotten when I noticed someone heading our way—it was Ryan

Baron. And it was too late for us to turn around.

"Oh, perfect," I muttered. Jenni squeezed my hand in anticipation.

"Hey, ladies," Ryan said as he reached us, his mouth forming into that annoying half smile of his. His short, dark blond hair was gelled as always, and he was wearing his standard white T-shirt and jeans.

"Hey," Jenni replied.

I didn't say a word. I just stood there with my arms crossed over my chest, waiting for Ryan to come out with his wise-guy remark.

I didn't have to wait long. "I'm terribly sorry you didn't win, Brennan," Ryan said, his half grin now turning into a full-fledged smile. "Better luck next time."

I rolled my eyes. "Thanks so much for your sincere support," I said sarcastically. "We'll just see how you manage next year, when you're dealing with a responsibility you don't even deserve to have."

"Whatever, Brennan." He shrugged. "That may be what you think, but the student body of Jefferson Memorial thinks otherwise." He fished around his pockets, extracting a bright pink flyer. "Anyway, this is for you guys," he said, handing the paper to Jenni. "Hope to see you there." Then he continued down the hall to wherever he was going. I shot daggers into his back with my eyes.

Jenni read the flyer aloud while I fumed: "Come

6

celebrate Ryan's presidency tonight at eight P.M. at the White House."

"Are you serious?" I asked, glancing over Jenni's shoulder at the invitation. Underneath the text was a Xerox of Ryan's house—which was indeed white.

"The ego on that guy!" I exclaimed, shaking my head. "Printing these invites up before even knowing if he was going to win! And to have the nerve to hand *us* an invite. As if we'd go!"

Jenni ripped up the flyer and threw it over our heads like confetti. "We wouldn't go to that loser's party if it was the last bash on earth. Now, c'mon, there's a sundae somewhere with our names on it."

"Yeah," I agreed. "Get me to Tastee-Freez *now*."

"So then Ryan gave this acceptance speech, and he was like, 'I promise to put back the "high" in Jefferson Memorial High,'" I recounted that evening, sitting around the dinner table with my mom, dad, and brother for what was supposed to have been my victory dinner—mashed potatoes, grilled chicken, and crescent rolls. My mom always took time out of her hectic schedule as a graphic designer to cook this—my favorite meal—when there was something to celebrate. But in this case she'd jumped the gun a little bit.

My father, a chiropractor who happens to bear a striking resemblance to David Letterman, pushed up his plaid sleeves and furrowed his eyebrows. "*High?* Was he talking about drugs?"

"No, Dad. High as in school's going to be such a

high now that he's president." I sighed. "And I'm not."

My mom's big blue eyes widened. "Obviously Ryan just tells people what they want to hear. You're clearly the best person for the job, sweetie."

I pushed my chicken around my plate dejectedly. "Then how come I lost?"

"Because life isn't always fair," my father said in a soothing tone, "and you can't expect to win every time."

"Dad's right," my mom agreed. "It's great that you're so motivated, but you have to learn not to be so hard on yourself. And you can't think of everything in terms of winning and losing. You did your best. That's all that matters."

"I guess," I said quietly. I knew that I often let my competitiveness get the better of me, but sometimes it just seemed impossible to control.

"Try to look at the bright side, Ky," my dad advised, placing down his fork. "Not being a class officer next year will free up a lot of time in your schedule. How many hours a week do you think you'd spend on presidential duties?"

"I don't know." I stared at the tall, melting candles in the middle of the table as I tried to calculate. "Maybe ten hours a week, give or take."

"So, let's think of this as a gift," he suggested. "You now have ten free hours a week with which you can do anything your heart desires. You could go mountain biking on the trails in the park. Go for hikes. Volunteer somewhere fun."

"Or you know how you love to run?" my mom

added. "You could start running in those free hours—before you know it, you could be entering the New York City Marathon."

My ten-year-old brother, Matthew, looked up from the mashed potato sculpture he'd been constructing for the past five minutes. "Want me to beat up this Ryan guy for you? I will, you know." He crossed his arms karate style above his plate. "I haven't been taking karate lessons for two years for nothing."

I smiled at my normally obnoxious brother's kind sentiment. "That's sweet, Matty, but I don't think Ryan's going to be intimidated by a ten-year-old karate kid. Although I do appreciate the offer."

"No sweat," he responded, demolishing his potato sculpture with his spoon and splattering some on his red T-shirt. "I'll kick his sorry butt."

"Matthew Brennan!" my mom reprimanded. "You're not going to kick anyone's butt."

"Don't give him a hard time, Mom," I said, standing up. "I'd like to kick Ryan's butt myself. But I think I'll go e-mail Stephanie instead." I excused myself from the table and headed to my bedroom.

Of the six other people who'd be on the Adventure Trails trip with me, Stephanie Hunt was the only one who'd e-mailed me so far. The trip leader, Wes, had given her my Web address when she'd registered for the trip a few months ago, and we'd been corresponding ever since.

I sat down at my hunter green desk and logged on, delighted to find that Stephanie was on-line as well. She instant-messaged me immediately: "Hey, Kylie! Am I talking to the new senior class president?"

I let out a long sigh as I typed: "Nope, unfortunately not. That jerk Ryan beat me."

"WHAT?" she asked in all caps. "He beat you? No way!"

"Way," I typed. I paused for a moment, realizing that right that second a very psyched Ryan Baron was having a victory party at his "white house"—with possibly a few of my own friends in attendance—while I was sitting in front of my Mac, totally bummed. Something was very wrong with this picture.

I shook those thoughts from my head and continued typing: "I don't mean to sound like a sore loser or anything, but it's hard to lose when you know a conceited jerk like him is the victor."

Stephanie typed the international symbol for sadness, :-(, then: "That blows. Let's just concentrate on the fun time we're going to have this summer. I can't wait to get out of New York City—even if it does mean going to Colorado for city girl rehab."

I laughed at her choice of words. Although I was going on the camping trip simply because I loved the outdoors, Stephanie's parents were sending her because they wanted her to broaden her Madison Avenue horizons and develop an appreciation for nature. "I'm ready to be there too," I typed. "Even though I'd rather be trapped in New York City than Oklahoma City any day of the week." It was hard for me to imagine how someone could get sick of living in the city that never sleeps.

"Yeah, I guess it could be worse," she typed.

"What's worse than anything is that I'm going to have to face Ryan tomorrow morning," I entered with a moan. "Just my luck, he's in five of my six classes."

"Ew! I don't envy you," she typed, punctuated by a :-(.

":-(for sure," I typed.

Two

I WOKE UP the next morning feeling a tight knot in the pit of my stomach. I'd had trouble falling asleep the night before, and when I did finally doze off after hours of tossing and turning, I'd been tormented by dreams of Ryan Baron.

Yawning, I slowly stepped out of bed and took a moment to stretch out my arms and legs and clear my thoughts. "Today's a new day," I told myself. "You have to put all this election business behind you."

I walked over to the window to check out the weather, and I smiled when I saw that it was sunny and bright outside. *It's almost summer—a fresh beginning,* I thought, walking over to my closet to pick out my clothes for the day. *Maybe you'll even go for a bike ride after school to gear up for Adventure Trails.*

By the time I'd pulled on my black cotton minidress, brushed my hair, and eaten a bowl of Special K and a banana, I was feeling a lot better.

I sang along to the radio as I drove to school, smiling widely and taking in all the sunshine as I pulled into the Jefferson Memorial parking lot. Sure, I wasn't too psyched to see Ryan that morning, but at least my junior year—filled with SATs, college research, and precalculus—was almost finally over, and my Adventure Trails trip was only weeks away. Backpack in hand, I shut the car door and strode across the parking lot, ready for summer to begin.

But my good mood evaporated as soon as I walked through Jefferson's heavy front doors. It was impossible to ignore the looks of pity everyone gave me as I made my way down the hallway to first period.

"Hey, Kylie," called Barbara, the editor of the yearbook. "It's so lame you didn't win."

"I voted for you," added her boyfriend, Rick.

"Too bad you couldn't have voted fifty times," I quipped with a smile.

To make matters worse, the apologetic looks and comments were intermingled with people raving about Ryan's party. As I passed a group of sophomore girls huddled around the water fountain, I heard them gush.

"Ryan's was the bomb," one of them said, while the others nodded in agreement.

"Definitely the best party this year," another girl added.

That was just what I needed to hear. I smiled weakly as a few more people offered their condolences. *You can do this,* I told myself as I continued down the hall, *just make it through one more week of school.*

But when Ryan walked up to me in homeroom, bubble gum cigar in hand, I felt like I was going to throw up. "Here, Brennan, have a chew on me," he said, his light blue eyes looking mischievous. Then he handed me one of his pastel cigars.

I glanced down at the faux cigar in my hand. The ring around it said I Won.

My shoulders stiffened. I felt like I was going to explode from annoyance. "Oh, *please,*" I told him, tossing the cigar into the garbage can. "How much money did you spend on these ridiculous victory prizes anyway?" Without waiting for his answer, I turned and headed toward my desk.

"What's the matter, Brennan?" he asked, following me. "Are you still all worked up 'cause you lost?"

I kept walking away from him without responding, letting out a deep breath and forcing myself to relax my shoulders. *Don't let him get to you,* I thought.

But he wouldn't let it go. "There's no need to be a sore loser," he taunted. "Hey, maybe we could talk Principal Overman into making you the student council *secretary.*"

That was it. I swung around to face him. "I wouldn't be a sore loser, Ryan, if you'd won fair and square. But you and I both know that you won't be able to deliver on even one of the

14

promises you made, you—you—lowdown snake!"

A superior smirk played on Ryan's lips. "Aw, Brennan, don't be that way. It's too bad there couldn't have been two winners, but there's no need to resort to name-calling. We're friends, right?"

I narrowed my eyes at him, then began to feel a little self-conscious when I realized that we were sparring in the middle of the classroom and that everyone was staring at us, waiting for my response. "Yeah, right, Ryan. With friends like you, who'd need enemies?"

The class oohed and ahhed at my retort. The bell rang before Ryan could respond. He just gave me an amused smile and walked to his desk.

I sank into my own wooden chair and glanced over at my friend Traci. She gave me the thumbs-up, but I still wasn't overly pleased that the entire class had witnessed Ryan and me fighting with each other.

As Mr. Devareux entered the room and promptly began to take attendance, my gaze focused through the glass door where Ryan's campaign poster, still tacked to the bulletin board in the hall, was clearly visible. It said Ryan Rules in bold red letters, with a picture of the face I loved to hate displayed right below it. In my opinion, the one thing that *ruled* about Ryan was that I wouldn't have to see him all summer.

"Baron?" Mr. Devareux called in his monotone voice.

"Here!" Ryan bellowed enthusiastically, as if

there was no other place he'd rather be.

As I responded "Here" after my name had been called, I thought about how there were a million places *I'd* rather be.

And all of them were far, far away from Ryan Baron.

"I can't believe junior year is over," Jenni said a week later, dropping into the desk next to mine in the final hour of school—current events. The only current event we were interested in today was our upcoming summer vacation, which was mere moments away. Before I had time to respond, the bell rang and Mr. Whitman, our teacher, walked in and called the class to order.

"Listen up, guys!" he called. "I've got good news and bad news." He waited until all our excited chatter died down before speaking again. "Here's the bad news: I know there's virtually no point in trying to teach in the last period of the last day of the school year. So the good news is that I'll let you all sign yearbooks until the bell rings."

This was a very well-received offer. The class erupted into hoots and hollers. Everyone extracted their yearbooks from their backpacks and desks and began to circulate them. We'd just received our yearbooks at lunch. I was too excited to even look through mine yet—I was saving it for when I got home and had the concentration to really read through it carefully.

"Well, I'm totally ready to move on with my

life," I said to Jenni. I glanced over at Ryan, who was looking through his yearbook with his close friend, Ben. "I just want to put this whole year behind me and look toward the future."

Jenni nodded. "I know—me too. I'm so psyched for my waitressing job at Cool Beans!"

"That will be fun," I agreed. "And while you're munching away on salsa and chips, I'll be camping in the open wild, eating fish I've caught, berries I've picked, the whole nine." I was smiling so widely at the thought of my trip that my cheeks began to hurt. "For eighteen days I'm going to be a full-out Girl Scout. I can't wait!"

Jenni laughed. "Sounds like torture to me. But I know *you'll* have a blast."

"Definitely! Even though I'll miss you in a major way."

"You liar!" she screeched. "You'll be too busy. But you better not be too busy to write me a few times while you're gone."

"You know I will," I promised, nodding.

Jenni pulled her yearbook out of her backpack and glanced through the pages. "I think I'll go ask Kerri to sign my book."

I looked around the classroom—most people were just acquaintances. Kerri was my only other good friend there. "I'll go with you," I told Jenni, following her to Kerri's side of the room.

As I autographed Kerri's and a few other people's books and everyone around me laughed and joked, I felt even more psyched than I had in weeks.

Summer would start in a half hour, I'd biked fifteen miles a day for seven days straight, and in two weeks I'd be off for the most incredible trip ever. Nothing could bring me down!

But perhaps I'd spoken too soon. Because when I turned around to see if there was anyone else in the class who I wanted to have sign my yearbook, I found Ryan standing right in front of me.

"Hey, Brennan," he said. "You wanna sign my yearbook?"

I blinked back at him for a moment, wondering if he was serious. First he played dirty to win the election, then he called me a sore loser, and now he wanted me to sign his yearbook? But as I stared back at his fake-innocent expression, I suddenly realized what he was up to—he probably just wanted to exchange yearbooks so that he could write in one final wise-guy remark before the year was through. That was just his style.

I nodded, smiling a saccharine-sweet grin. I'd sign his book, all righty, but it wasn't going to be pretty. "Okay, Ryan, sure," I said.

"Cool," he said, that half smile of his forming on his lips. Yup, he was definitely up to no good.

We exchanged books, and I sat down at my desk to figure out what I should write. I had a good idea of the sorts of things that Ryan would scribble in my yearbook—how he beat me out, how he was number one, and how much better he was than I. Well, I'd show him.

I picked up my pen, struck by sudden inspiration. I wrote slowly:

Dear Ryan,

You may have beat me out in the election, but you and I both know I was the best person for the job. Go ahead—pass out your bubble gum cigars and throw your parties and act like you rule the world. But everyone knows that truth wins out in the end. When you fail to deliver Fiona, or bands in the caf, or free b-day absences, how many supporters will you have then? I'm sure it will be zero. And when that day comes, I will laugh and laugh and laugh.

Dying of suspense,
Kylie Brennan

I signed my name with a flourish, even dotting my *i* with a heart. I usually didn't get pleasure out of trashing people in their own yearbooks, but I was sure Ryan's message would be even meaner than mine was. I didn't feel bad in the least—he deserved it.

I was smiling to myself, rereading my note, when Ryan came over and handed me my book, snatching his out of my hands. "Well, Brennan, have a good summer," he said.

"Yeah, you too," I responded, knowing that my summer was going to be more than perfect, especially since he wouldn't be around to ruin it.

I flipped through my yearbook as Ryan walked

away, finding his note to me on the very last page. I read quickly, expecting the worst.

> Dear Kylie,
> You were a great opponent, and you gave me a real run for my money. You had an awesome platform, and I hope we can put our heads together next year and work together on a few projects. Have a great summer.
>
> See you next year,
> Ryan Baron

My head spinning, I slammed my yearbook shut. What could have possessed Ryan to write such an uncharacteristic message? It was actually . . . *nice!* I suddenly felt a twinge of guilt for writing such a rude note to him. But as I glanced at Ryan across the room and saw him laughing hysterically with Ben, all the sarcastic quips and mean remarks that Ryan had said over the years came rushing back to me. I immediately lost all feelings of guilt—Ryan Baron was simply incapable of being nice. Obviously Ryan wanted to make me feel bad by making it look like *I* was the one with the attitude problem while he was the nice one. What was that old saying? Kill 'em with kindness. I nodded to myself. I was sure that was what Ryan was trying to do. Well, that wasn't going to work on me. No way, José.

The final bell rang, interrupting my internal monologue. I jumped up—summer was here! I shook off any weird feelings I had about Ryan's note as I gathered up my things.

Jenni ran over to me and picked up her bag. "Happy summer, Ky!" she hollered, grabbing me in a hug.

"You too, Jen," I said, hugging her back.

"What was up with Ryan?" she whispered as we disconnected. "I saw you guys signing each other's yearbooks."

I shook my head, rolling my eyes. "Just more of the same."

Jenni raised her eyebrows in curiosity. "Oh? What did he say?"

I opened my mouth to answer her, then closed it again. "You know what?"

"What?"

I smiled. "Let's not talk about Ryan. Because he's now officially out of my life for three whole months!"

Three

TWO WEEKS LATER I walked off the plane in Colorado, so excited I could barely stand it. My adventure of a lifetime was about to begin! Despite the fact that I'd been sad saying good-bye to Jenni at the airport and that I'd been trapped next to a screaming little kid on the long airplane ride over, I was beyond thrilled to be here.

I scanned the crowd as I walked, spotting a Welcome Home, Grandma! sign and a Congrats, Boulder Wildcats banner. Then I spied a guy in khaki shorts standing off to the left, waving a sign that said Adventure Trails—Kylie. Enthusiasm building, I ran over to him, figuring he had to be Wes, the trip leader I'd made all the arrangements with over the phone. With his brown hair, tan skin, and tall build, he looked exactly like I'd pictured him to. The only thing about him that surprised me was his age. He looked like he was twenty-seven or twenty-eight—at least five years younger than I'd guessed he'd be.

I waved wildly as I neared him. "You must be Wes," I said, extending my free hand.

"And you must be Kylie Brennan," he said. He was definitely pretty cute—sort of like an outdoorsy Clark Kent. "You're our fourth camper to arrive so far today."

I smiled, thinking about how I couldn't wait to meet the others. This was going to be awesome!

We made our way to the baggage claim, and Wes reiterated some of the trip information that had been outlined in the Adventure Trails brochure. We were to spend four days at the base camp in Granite, Colorado, which was about fifteen minutes away, learning and practicing basic camping skills. Then we were going to camp for two weeks in the backwoods of Yellowstone National Park, where we'd backpack, canoe, rock climb, mountain bike, and white-water raft.

"It sounds incredible!" I exclaimed, keeping my eyes peeled for my bright red backpack on the conveyor belt.

"Yeah, it is," Wes said. "At least most people think so. Although occasionally we get a few city types who think it's anything but fun."

I laughed, thinking of Stephanie. I sure hoped she could hack it in the great outdoors. From her e-mails, though, she sounded like she was more into clubbing than camping. "Stephanie Hunt is definitely a city girl," I said. I spotted my overstuffed backpack and reached out for it.

Wes helped me lift my bag off the conveyor

belt. "That's actually who I was thinking of," he told me. "Stephanie arrived this morning, and I think she's experiencing a bit of a culture shock. You two have been e-mailing, right?"

I nodded as I squared my heavy bag on my shoulders, thinking of all Steph and I had shared over the Internet: our mutual addiction to *Ally McBeal* and *Party of Five,* our plans for where we wanted to go to college, our hopes of meeting cute guys on the trip, our respective types (hers— tall, dark, and handsome; mine—blond, blue-eyed, and tan), and many other equally important tidbits. "We've had a great cyberfriendship," I said, following Wes out to the parking lot. "I can't wait to meet her face-to-face."

"Well, you only have about fifteen more minutes till you do." He stopped in front of a Chevy Suburban. "This is us. We'll be at the camp in no time." Wes took my bag from me and threw it in the back. I jumped into the passenger seat.

On the ride to Granite, I was spellbound by the immense mountains that surrounded the land. I'd never seen anything like them—they were so beautiful and so *large.* I reached over to the backseat and fished out my camera from my backpack. I took a picture out the window as we drove, wanting to remember this moment—and the feeling the mountains evoked in me—forever.

Before I knew it, we were pulling up to base camp. Wes parked next to a huge log cabin. It was practically the size of my house. Hundreds of trees and lots of smaller cabins surrounded it, like something out of a storybook.

"Ohmigosh, it's gorgeous," I said. Since I'd grown up in Oklahoma City, where the land is pretty much flat and lifeless, I was blown away by the lush terrain of the campsite.

"I know, it really is amazing here," Wes said, walking around back to retrieve my bag. "Home, sweet home."

I smiled, realizing that this *was* my sweet home, at least for the next few days. I stood still for a moment, inhaling the crisp mountain air and closing my eyes, listening to the birds chirping. I felt the afternoon sun beat down on my face. This was heaven, plain and simple. It was everything I'd dreamed of and more. And the trip hadn't even really started yet.

I opened my eyes and saw a red-haired girl throw open the door of the lodge. She rushed toward us. "Kylie," Wes said. "Meet Stephanie."

We squealed and hugged each other like long-lost friends. "Oh, wow, it's so cool to meet you!" Stephanie exclaimed, her voice shrill.

"I feel like I know you even though we've never met," I said, pulling back to get a good look at my friend. She was tall—about five-foot-ten, with long red hair and green eyes. Stephanie's city style showed—she was decked out in a black formfitting tank top and fitted black shorts. She looked like she just stepped off the Eddie Bauer runway or something—campsite chic.

I heard the lodge door open again. I looked over and saw a supercute guy emerge from the main cabin. "Isn't he hot?" Stephanie whispered. "I think he's your type."

I stared at the guy who was approaching us. He definitely *was* my type, no doubt about that. He had long blond hair, a dark tan, and a tall, lanky body clothed in a green T-shirt and khaki shorts.

"Dirk," Stephanie said when he reached us, "this is the girl I was telling you about: Kylie Brennan."

"Hi," I said. My eyes were so fixed on him that it took me a moment to get the word out.

He flashed me a perfect white grin. "Nice to meet you," he said.

An athletic-looking girl with short brown hair and sparkling green eyes bounced out from the lodge. "Hi, I'm Sue," she said, extending a hand. "But please call me Betty."

Perplexed, I took my gaze off Dirk for a moment. "Huh?" I asked Sue/Betty. "How come?"

"My friends call me Betty, as in snow betty, because I'm addicted to snowboarding," she explained.

"That's pretty original," I told her, smiling. I'd never snowboarded before, but Betty, with her lean frame and Nike athletic wear, looked like she was probably a pro. In fact, she looked so cut and fit that I had a sudden worry she might outshine me on the trip. I fought the twinge of competitiveness that was threatening to rise inside me. *This trip isn't a competition,* I thought, taking a deep breath. Even though I would have loved to be the best athlete

26

there, it wasn't like the world would end if I wasn't.

"Well, let's get Kylie to her cabin," Wes suggested. "You want to show her, Steph?"

Stephanie nodded. "Aren't we sleeping in this big cabin right here?" I asked.

"That's what I thought, Kylie," Dirk told me. "But that's just the main cabin, with the dining room and stuff. We're all in those smaller ones down the way."

Wes handed me my backpack. "Here you go," he said, wiping his palms on the front of his shorts. "Now, I guess I'm off to collect the other campers. They're all coming in on the same connecting flight. Feel free to settle into your cabins or hang out in the lodge. Just be sure to meet back here with your day pack and canteen in about thirty minutes." He started to walk away, then turned back. "Oh, like I told some of you earlier, be sure to put on some insect repellant. The mosquitoes are rampant this time of year. It's not a good idea to be outside without some protection."

I slapped my arm, already feeling a bite. "Will do."

Dirk looked over at me, and I felt my heart melt like an ice cube in Tahiti. "Are you sure you don't need a hand with that bag?" he asked, a southern drawl now apparent in his voice.

I wondered where he was from. I also wondered if I should let him carry my bag. It was tempting, the thought of being able to spend some more time getting to know him, but I'd never been the type to

27

let a guy do things for me. I was quite capable of carrying my own bag. Besides, there'd be plenty of time to hang out with him later. "No thanks," I answered, lifting my pack onto my shoulders.

"All right," Dirk answered. "But you ladies give a holler if you need a hand."

"Thanks," Stephanie responded. "Catch you guys later. Kylie, our cabin's this way."

"Okay," I said, watching Dirk disappear into the main cabin before following Stephanie along the dirt trail.

"I am so psyched to finally meet you in person!" Stephanie exclaimed.

"I'm excited too," I said. "It's weird to finally be here. I've been looking forward to it for so long, I can hardly believe it's finally happening."

Steph laughed, veering toward the first cabin on the left. "Well, being somewhere without taxicabs and skyscrapers is a total shock to my system." She opened the screen door. "Here we are," she said.

I entered the musty cabin and was immediately brought back to Camp Wanakawa, sixth grade. There were twin bunk beds, hardwood floors, and a beat-up chest of drawers in the corner. "I stayed in a cabin just like this when I was twelve, only ours had a lot more beds," I told Steph, my brain suddenly flooded with memories. I dropped my bag and collapsed onto the bed. "I had my first kiss that summer. Danny Franklin." I smiled. "He kept his eyes open the whole time."

Stephanie sat down next to me. "Well, then this is too weird."

"What's too weird?" I asked.

"All these coincidences. This is the same type of cabin as that camp. And you kissed Danny Franklin," she said, weighing each word with this mysterious importance.

"And?"

"Don't you see?" She shook her head. "Danny Franklin. Dirk Frazier."

I stared back at her blankly. What on earth was she talking about?

"Same initials, silly!" she explained. "My mom makes a living on stuff like this. It's in the stars!"

I nodded, remembering that Stephanie's mom wrote a nationally syndicated horoscope column. "I know your mom's an expert on that moon-and-the-stars stuff, but I think you're reading a little too much into this." I fell back on the bed. "Even though Dirk *is* a total babe."

"I knew you would think he was hot!" Stephanie told me, jumping up. "I would too, but he's not really my type. Plus he looks a lot like my older brother, Scott. That ruins it for me completely."

I tried to imagine kissing someone who looked like an older version of Matthew. That would definitely gross me out.

"Anyway," Stephanie continued, "Dirk seems pretty cool. He's from Texas, and he's seventeen."

I laughed. "Thanks for doing the background check for me." I sat up straight. "Well, I'm almost seventeen, and Texas does border Oklahoma," I said, already mentally planning our long-distance relationship. "But do you think Betty is into him?"

"No way," Stephanie answered. "I didn't detect any vibes between them at all, and I hung with them all morning. No exchanged glances, no hair flips, nothing."

"I hope you're right. I'd hate to have to steal him from under her snowboarding nose," I joked.

Stephanie laughed. "There's no stopping you, huh?"

I shook my head. "Not really."

"I'm surprised you've never had a boyfriend before with that attitude," she commented. "But you seem like you're kinda picky."

I stood up, stretching out my legs. "I suppose I am," I admitted. "I've just never met a guy who's come up to my boyfriend standards. *Yet.* But that could all change with Dirk."

"I hope so," Steph told me. "Hey," she said, playing with a strand of her hair, "how come you didn't let him carry your bag for you? That would have been prime flirting time."

I walked over to my backpack and pulled out a hair band. "'Cause," I told her, gathering my hair up into a ponytail, "I feel uncomfortable when guys do things like that for me. I mean, I can carry my own bag—I'm just as strong as lots of guys are."

"I don't doubt it. But if it were me . . ." Stephanie smiled as her voice trailed off. "Well, I don't mind when guys act kind of chivalrous, you know?" She glanced down at her watch. "Anyway, let me give you a tour of the cabin, then let's go back to the lodge. I want a front-row seat when the rest of the campers arrive."

"Okeydokey." I followed Steph as she showed me the closet, the tiny bathroom, and the back porch.

I glanced out the screen window and noticed that there was a little bluebird sitting out on the ledge looking in at us. "Don't you think this is the most perfect place?" I sighed. "I could live here forever."

Stephanie looked around the cabin warily. "Forever's a long time. And this place is a far cry from my loft in SoHo. But I *am* going to make a major effort to appreciate its rustic charm while I'm here. And I've got the coolest roomie in the land, which is a total plus."

"That's for sure," I agreed, gazing at the trees right outside our cabin. I opened the screen door and stepped out for a moment. The sun had started to lower in the sky—it looked as though it was sitting on the majestic mountains in the distance.

"Steph," I called to her inside, "I have a feeling that this is going to be one incredible summer."

Four

NIGHT WAS BEGINNING to fall by the time we walked out of our cabin and headed back up the dirt trail. In the distance I could make out Wes's Suburban fast approaching. "Perfect timing," I said.

"Yep." Stephanie began to walk faster. "I can't wait to meet everyone else."

"Me either." As I sped up to match Stephanie's pace I couldn't help scanning the scene for Dirk. I looked around for the blond hair, the tan, built body, the Colgate smile. But they weren't anywhere to be found.

The Suburban pulled to a stop by the main cabin. "Looks like one of those guys could be cute," Steph said, checking out the new campers' emerging forms.

"It's hard to tell from here." I squinted to get a better look. I saw what looked like one blond guy, one brown-haired guy, and one blond girl piling out from the vehicle.

"No, the darker one definitely looks cute," Stephanie insisted. "I'm from New York, so I'm used to checking out guys from far away. You know, like in crowds."

"I wouldn't exactly call four people a crowd," I said.

"I'm not saying it's a crowd," Stephanie whispered. "I'm just saying they're far away. But getting closer by the minute."

By the time we were close enough to actually discern any of the new people's features, all we could see were the backs of their heads. They were all busy getting their bags out of the back of the Chevy. The guy that Stephanie thought looked cute had pretty much disappeared from view altogether—he was leaning into the backseat, apparently searching for something.

"Hey, guys," Wes called, waving us over, "I'd like you to meet our latest arrivals." The light-haired guy and the girl were standing beside him, backpacks in hand. "Tyson and Daisy, meet Stephanie and Kylie."

Tyson had strawberry blond hair, a wrestler's stocky body, and freckles like my little brother. Daisy, with her long blond hair, tie-dyed jumper, and Birkenstock sandals, looked like the classic granola girl. Steph and I shook their hands and welcomed them to the campsite.

"I still can't find them," a muffled voice called from the backseat.

"Lost his sunglasses," Wes explained. "Don't

worry about it—I'm sure we'll find them later. Come meet some of the campers," he called back.

The last camper stepped out of the Suburban.

"Kylie and Stephanie," Wes said, "I'd like you—"

My jaw dropped to the ground.

"Oh. My. God," I whispered. I felt like I was going to throw up. "This can't be happening."

"—to meet Ryan," Wes finished.

It took me a second to understand that I was *really* staring right into the eyes of Ryan Baron.

"Ryan!" I gasped, my stomach twisting in circles. This had to be some sort of evil joke.

Ryan looked just as shocked as I felt. His light blue eyes were wide with surprise. "Brennan?" he said. "What are you doing here?"

"What am *I* doing here?" I asked. "What are *you* doing here?"

"You two know each other?" Wes asked.

"Yeah," Ryan and I said in unison.

"Small world, seeing as you're from Iowa and she's from Oklahoma," Wes was saying to Ryan. But I barely heard him—my mind was too busy reeling with anger. In one fell swoop Ryan Baron had managed to ruin my entire summer. It was like I couldn't escape the guy. My whole body stiffened. This was going to be torture!

"My dad's from Iowa, and that's where I was for the week," Ryan explained, surprise still evident in his voice. "But I go to school in Oklahoma. With Kylie."

"Yeah, we go to school together," I said, nudging

34

Stephanie in hopes that she'd make the connection.

"Oh," she said softly. "Ryan *from school.*"

I glanced over at her for consolation, but she was busy looking Ryan up and down. I almost wanted to apologize to her for Ryan's presence, as if it was somehow my fault that he was here. Ryan was sure to be an annoyance to everyone on the trip. But I had no doubt that I was the one who would suffer the most.

"Talk about fate," Daisy commented.

At that moment Dirk and Betty burst through the lodge doors, faces flushed. Not even the sight of Dirk's gorgeous face could lift me out of the depths of depression that I was now buried in. I wondered if there was some way I could get a refund on this trip.

"He beat me in Ping-Pong, three games to two," Betty said, rushing over to us.

"Yeah, but she's quite a player," Dirk said. He grinned at me, and I tried to smile back, but it was the last thing I felt like doing at the moment.

Wes called us all to attention and made the final introductions. As everyone chatted excitedly I cast my eyes down to the dirt, trying to deny that this was happening to me.

"Okay, guys, listen up," Wes bellowed. "Here are your cabin assignments: Ryan, you're rooming with Dirk; Tyson, you're with me; and Daisy's with Betty." As Wes paused I thought about how lame it was that my worst enemy was rooming with my latest crush. I was certain that

35

Ryan would poison Dirk with horrible lies about me. My luck was getting worse by the second. "Ryan, Tyson, and Daisy," Wes continued, "follow me to your cabins to unload your bags and put on some insect repellant. As I've told the rest of the group, mosquitoes are ruthless this time of year, so the repellant is mandatory. Everyone else head to the kitchen and gather up buns, hot dogs, marshmallows, and paper plates for our welcome campfire."

The group cheered, and a flurry of activity ensued as everyone followed Wes's orders. I didn't move. I stood motionless, still completely shell-shocked. *This is all just a nightmare,* I told myself as I watched Ryan walk down the dirt trail. *You'll wake up in a minute, and it will be over.*

A sudden voice in my ear shattered my catatonic state, bringing me back to reality.

"So that's the Ryan who won the election?" Stephanie whispered.

"The one and only," I answered, my heart sinking. "This is horrible. I can't believe this is happening."

Stephanie began to lead me toward the main cabin. "I think you're going to kill me," she said quietly.

I took my eyes off the ground and looked up at her. "Why? Did you invite him here or something?" I joked.

"No." Steph shook her head. "But . . ." A guilty expression appeared on her face. "Well, I think Ryan is really cute," she told me.

I stopped short. "What?" I exclaimed.

"I'm sorry," she said, shrugging. "I can't help it. He seemed sorta cool."

"Whatever." I shook my head in disbelief. "You'll find out soon enough that he's anything *but* cool."

"Maybe," Steph responded. "But hey, do you know if he has a girlfriend or anything?"

I blinked back at her. Was she *joking?* "I feel like I'm in the twilight zone or something. First Ryan Baron appears on my supposed-to-be-perfect trip, then you start acting like you're interested in him. . . ." My voice trailed off as my brain got lost in the ridiculousness of it all.

"Listen, Kylie, I don't want to upset you," Steph said, looking concerned. "I won't go for Ryan or anything if you don't want me to. I wouldn't want to jeopardize our friendship over this."

I regarded Steph, thinking her comment over for a moment. Her forehead was creased into a worried line, and her green eyes searched my face.

I can't tell her who to like, I realized, sighing heavily. *And I can't be mad at her if she's interested in Ryan . . . even if it is the stupidest thing I ever heard.*

"No, don't stop liking him on my account," I told her. "I have no clue what you'd find cute about him, but it's a free country. Besides, pretty soon you'll see what an annoying jerk he is and you'll lose all interest."

Steph gave me a spontaneous hug. "You're the

best!"

I smiled weakly. "Yeah, well, all I can say is spare me the details if anything *does* happen with Ryan. If you guys end up kissing or something, I just might puke."

Steph laughed. "We'll see about that. C'mon, let's go join the rest of the crew inside."

"You go ahead," I told her. "I need a minute to collect myself. I'll be right in."

"You okay?" Steph frowned.

I nodded. "Yeah, I'll be fine. I just need to chill out here for a sec."

"Cool," Steph responded. "See you in a minute." And then she jogged into the main cabin.

I walked over to the cabin's front steps and plopped down, exhausted from the mental anguish this past hour had caused me. I rested my head in my hands, thinking, *Why me, why me? Of all the Adventure Trails trips Ryan could've chosen, why did he have to choose this one?*

Filled with frustration, I tilted my head back and looked up at the sky. It was now completely dark, and for the first time that evening I realized that the sky was blanketed with bright, twinkling stars. It was amazing—there were so many dots of bright light above that I felt like I was in *Star Trek* or something. It didn't take me long to spot most of the constellations. I realized I could spend hours staring up at the vast night sky—I could lose myself in the infinite stars.

I smiled and closed my eyes, enjoying the feel of

the slightly cool breeze in my hair. This *was the reason I came on this trip,* I reminded myself. *The mountains, fresh air, millions of stars—you can't let Ryan ruin all that for you.* Yes, I thought, nodding, *just ignore Ryan and appreciate all the awesome things you're going to do.*

At that moment the group's laughter from inside the main cabin reached my ears. *And there are plenty of cool people on this trip—Steph is great.* I stood up and brushed the dirt off my shorts. *And Dirk is superhot. He just might be your dream man.*

I opened the front door to the cabin. *Ryan or no Ryan,* I thought, *this is still going to be the best summer ever!*

With that energizing thought I ran inside and found myself in the middle of a cozy room equipped with a fireplace, a large, worn-looking plaid couch, a couple of chairs, and a Ping-Pong table in the corner.

I followed the sound of the voices and walked toward the right, which led me through a dining room with a very long picnic table decorated with a couple of small vases of wildflowers. I walked up to a pair of swinging wooden doors and pushed them open.

"Hey, there," Betty called as I entered the huge kitchen.

"There you are!" Dirk said. "I was just about to send out a search party."

I laughed—I couldn't have been outside longer than three minutes. But his concern was sweet nonetheless. "I was taking in the sights," I said. "You know, just enjoying being out here."

"Good for you. That's what we all should be doing," Dirk said, giving me an adorable wink.

I smiled, noticing that he had a cute dimple in his left cheek. Yup, his presence almost made up for Ryan being here. *Almost.*

"So what do we need to do?" I asked.

"Well, we were just screwing around until you got here. But I guess we should divvy this up," Dirk said, looking at the list Wes had left on the kitchen table. "Kylie, you find the hot dogs and the condiments. Steph, grab the buns. Betty, paper plates. And I'll get the marshmallows. Then we should be all set."

A take-charge kind of guy—I liked that. We all started looking through the cabinets for our various items. I stuck my head in the stainless steel fridge in search of the hot dogs. "Beef, turkey, and veggie," I recited, looking at the packages. "Any preference?"

"I vote for veggie," Steph responded, reaching for a bag of buns.

"Better bring them all," Dirk said. "But I'm a turkey man, myself."

"Me too," I said, delighted to find that we had something in common.

"You're a turkey man too?" Dirk teased, pulling three bags of marshmallows from an open cabinet.

"A turkey *woman*," I corrected him, "thank you very much."

Stephanie caught my eye and winked. I guessed it was obvious to her as well that there was some good chemistry between Dirk and me.

Betty plopped the package of paper plates on the table. "I'll take beef any day," she said. "We're gonna need our strength, according to my boyfriend. He took this exact same trip last year and told me to load up on the proteins."

Suddenly there was the sound of feet stomping and voices chatting—the rest of the crew had entered the lodge.

I groaned inwardly as I made out Ryan's voice over the others. *Keep it under control,* I reminded myself, taking the ketchup and mustard out of the fridge. *Forget about him.*

But I couldn't ignore the sinking feeling that overcame me when I saw Ryan walk into the kitchen with the rest of the group a moment later. My only consolation was that Ryan was looking equally uncomfortable at the sight of me. When we made eye contact, he cast his gaze away from me quickly and looked at Dirk instead. "Hey, we all set?" he asked.

Dirk nodded. "Plates, marshmallows, dogs, and buns, all present and accounted for."

"The makings of an excellent feast," Ryan commented, rubbing his hands together. "I'm starved. All I've had all day is an airplane sandwich, which didn't quite do it for me."

Stephanie made a face. "I know, plane food's the worst."

"Okay, then everybody grab something and put it in your day pack," Wes instructed. "And be sure to fill up your canteens if you haven't already. We're going to hike to a campsite about a mile away, then have our cookout."

I stuck the paper plates in my pack and stood in line behind Steph to fill my canteen, excited about the upcoming journey.

To my dismay, Ryan filed in behind me. "Pretty weird that we're on the same trip, huh?" he said, tapping me on the shoulder.

"Yeah," I said, "small world."

"And I bet you're just so glad to see me," he said in a sarcastic tone as I stepped up to the sink.

I rolled my eyes. "Oh? Why do you think that?"

"Because now you'll have a guy to set up your tent and protect you out in the wilderness," he teased. "I'm not just brains, you know. I'm quite an outdoorsman—I can help you with anything you can't do."

"Please," I responded, annoyance creeping up my spine.

"What's the matter, Brennan?" Ryan went on. "Afraid that I might outdo you in the athletic department too?"

My hands tightened with anger around my water bottle. Then I was struck by a brilliant idea. I stepped to the right, placed my fingers directly on the faucet head, and "accidentally" sprayed Ryan with water.

"Hey!" Ryan yelped in surprise.

"Oops," I said innocently. "Didn't mean to getcha."

42

"You okay over there?" Wes called, eyeing us curiously.

"Don't worry," I said in a mock-girlish tone. "I've got big bad Ryan to come to my rescue." Then under my breath, so only Ryan could hear, I muttered, "Sexist pig," and stomped off.

"What's up?" Steph asked as I approached her and Wes by the swinging doors of the kitchen. "Did you get wet?"

"Just a little," I said, brushing myself off. "But it was worth it."

I looked over at Ryan, who was shaking his head, trying to dry off. I wasn't exactly doing a good job of not letting Ryan get to me. But, I thought with a smile, spraying that water on him sure felt good.

The one-mile hike to the campsite was a breeze for me. But Steph, whose brand-new Timberland boots hadn't been broken in yet, was having a hard time keeping up. After she insisted it was okay with her, I picked up my pace and began to hike a few feet behind Wes on the tree-lined trail. It was pretty dark by now, so we all carried flashlights as we made our way to the campsite. And the crescent moon illuminated the trail with its glow.

I realized that imagining this sort of hike and scenery was what had gotten me through the end of junior year and the loss of the election. Of course, Ryan hadn't been part of my fantasies—except for the ones where I wished he'd get hit by a bus—but even still, reality was pretty close to my dreams. I took a deep breath, trying to cram as much fresh air as I possibly could into my lungs.

"What are you thinking about?" Dirk asked me.

I turned my head, startled. I'd been so lost in my own thoughts that I hadn't realized he'd caught up with me. "Just how happy I am to be here."

"Me too," Dirk responded. "Texas is beautiful, but it's nothing like Colorado. The mountains are incredible. It sure beats staring at the Dallas skyline. Even though that takes my breath away too if the time is right."

"And when's that?"

"When the setting sun's hitting the mirrored buildings just so," Dirk explained, "and it looks like a pink and orange and purple rainbow exploded all over them."

"Sounds amazing," I remarked. "Oklahoma City doesn't have much of a skyline. It's mainly flat all over."

"That can be beautiful too," Dirk said. "This whole country's gorgeous in its own way, if you know how to appreciate it."

"I take it you do?" I teased.

"Sure," he said, smiling. "Be where you are. Savor the beauty around you. Like right now. There's nowhere on earth I'd rather be than on this trail with these trees around me and these crunchy leaves below me and the mountains in the distance, talking to a girl like you."

I blushed, not knowing how to respond. "That's so sweet," I said finally, willing myself to remember

44

his words so I could report them to Stephanie later.

At that moment Stephanie joined us, out of breath. "Hey guys, where's the fire? Get it? Where's the fire, as in why are you walking so fast, and where's the fire, as in we are about to learn how to build a fire."

"Very funny," I said, laughing despite myself. I glanced back and saw that Betty, Tyson, Ryan, and Daisy were chatting and hiking maybe twenty feet behind us. I wondered if Ryan had gotten to any of them yet. "How are the boots?"

"Absolutely killing me." Stephanie moaned, leaning down to rub her heel. "We're talking blister city."

Wes looked back at us. "Steph, your dogs still barking? We need to apply some ointment on your blisters when we get there. We don't want your feet to get infected."

"Okay," she said, shrugging. "Guess I should've worn these boots a few times before today, huh?"

"I'm sure you'll be fine once you get in the swing of things. If you ever need to stop and give your feet a rest, just say so. But here we are anyway," Wes said, pointing to an upcoming clearing illuminated by the moonlight, covered with leaves and twigs. "Steph, have a seat and take off those boots. Everybody else, sit down in a circle formation while we get Steph fixed up."

"I'm okay, I'm okay," Steph protested. "I want to help build the fire."

"Let's just get a Band-Aid or two on those blisters," Wes insisted, "and then it will be back to business as usual."

"Okay, I give," Steph said, sitting down on a tree stump and untying her boots.

We all settled in as Wes handed Stephanie a first aid kit from his day pack and showed her how to dress her blisters. "All right, guys, while Stephanie gets her feet fixed up, let's get cracking on Campfire 101."

He clapped and sat down at the head of our circle. "First of all," he began, "it's always good to carry a ready supply of wooden matches—or better yet a butane lighter—while you're camping. But tonight we're going to use the good old rubbing-two-sticks-together method."

"Awesome!" Daisy exclaimed. "Like we're one with nature."

"I'd rather use a Bic lighter and remain two with nature," Stephanie said, looking up from her bandages.

We all chuckled at Steph's comment, our laughter echoing in the warm night air. Wes waited for us to quiet down before continuing. "First, we need to collect dried tree bark, pinecones, and needles to use as tinder. This is what we'll use to light bigger pieces of wood for the fire."

"How do we know what kind of tinder to pick up?" Tyson asked, looking at the twigs covering the ground all around us.

"Tinder's essentially starter fuel, so just make sure it falls into one of the categories I mentioned,"

Wes explained. "And it's got to be dry. If it's not dry, it's useless." Wes stood up, aiming his flashlight to the ground. "Let's start by gathering dry tinder and placing it in a pile right here. Once that's done, we'll move on to the bigger stuff."

We all got up and collectively brushed the dirt off our backsides. "I hope these shorts don't stain," Stephanie said, walking over to me. "They're J. Crew."

I laughed as I began to search the ground with my flashlight. "I think you're gonna have to accept the fact that your clothes *will* get dirty on this trip."

Steph bent over. "I suppose you're right," she said. Then she stood back up, a couple of pinecones in her hands. "Hey, you and Dirk really seem to be hitting it off."

"Shhh," I said, looking around to make sure Dirk wasn't within earshot, although it was too dark out to tell. "I know," I whispered back. "He's definitely making this whole Ryan thing easier for me to swallow."

"Good to hear," Steph said.

"Hey, Brennan," Ryan suddenly called out from the darkness. My neck stiffened at the sound of his voice.

He became visible as he approached us with his flashlight. Then he shone it right in my face. The bright light momentarily blinded me. "Hey!" I exclaimed. "I can't see."

"So *sorry*," Ryan said sarcastically. He aimed the flashlight back to the ground and walked up closer to Steph and me. "But I can't help noticing that those hands of yours seem to be empty. Looks like I'm schooling you in tinder collecting this evening."

"Yeah?" I put my hands on my hips. "For your information, I already dumped a big heap of tinder onto the pile," I lied, nudging Steph so that she'd play along. There was no way I was going to let Ryan think that he was beating me already. "Steph and I are beginning our second collection, so *you* have some catching up to do." I shone my flashlight on his arms—he was carrying a bunch of tinder in his left arm. "All you have is that measly pile."

"Yeah," Steph said, giggling. "We're clearly number one in tinder collecting so far."

"Well," Ryan responded. "My mistake. You two are really a couple of tough women."

Steph giggled again. I couldn't help rolling my eyes at both the sarcasm in Ryan's voice and the flirtatious sound of Steph's laughter. She was actually *flirting* with Ryan Baron. *Ugh*.

"Okay," Wes hollered, thankfully rescuing me out of that annoying moment. "Looks like enough tinder. Now, time for the kindling." He shone the flashlight on his face as he spoke. "Look for dried twigs and pieces of wood no more than an inch thick. But rather than pile them up like you did with the tinder, you want to lay the kindling in a crisscross fashion. Build it up like a tepee, making sure to stack it loosely. This will let air in to fan the fire."

"Will you show us how?" Betty asked. "I'm having trouble picturing it."

"Sure," Wes said. "I'll hang out here by the tinder so when you bring your kindling over, I'll walk you all through it."

"You ladies need a lesson on finding twigs?" Ryan asked Steph and me.

Steph giggled yet again. I decided to take this opportunity to get as far away from the two of them as possible. I really liked Steph and all, but I couldn't just stand there as she flirted with my worst enemy.

"I'll go my own way, thanks," I told Ryan. "I think we'll find that I'll be teaching you a thing or two."

"Oooh," I heard Ryan retort as I turned and walked away.

Flashlight down, I hurriedly searched for twigs, determined to collect more than Ryan. *Does he just think he's the best person on earth?* I thought angrily, collecting twig after twig. *Well, I'll show him! I'll show him who's—*

"Need some help?" Dirk asked, coming up beside me and pulling me out of my angry thoughts. "You have quite a load there."

"No!" I exclaimed, taken aback. What was with the guys on this trip? Did they think every female was helpless?

"Sorry," Dirk said, sounding offended. "I was trying to help."

Luckily it was too dark out there for Dirk to notice my cheeks flush with embarrassment. I

49

sighed. He was simply being nice. I had let Ryan get to me, and I was taking it out on Dirk. "No, I'm sorry. It was sweet of you to offer. I was mad about something else—I wasn't thinking."

"That's cool," Dirk responded. "But I take it you can manage all right?"

I smiled. "Yes, thanks. But please ignore my psychotic response."

"No problem," he told me. "I find psychotic behavior quite attractive in girls."

My knees turned to jelly. We had some serious chemistry going on. "Really?" I picked up a couple more twigs. "How interesting."

"Shall we bring our wood over to the pile?" Dirk suggested.

"We shall," I agreed, tingling with excitement. Not only was Dirk cute, but he'd managed to take my mind off Ryan and calm me down.

After everyone gave their wood to Wes, he demonstrated how to stack it over the kindling. It was much simpler than he'd made it sound—it sort of looked like a pyramid.

"Okay, once the tinder and kindling are in place, you want to light the tinder," Wes explained. "Shine your flashlights here so I can show you. Get two dry sticks, about an inch in diameter, and rub them together like so." He grabbed the sticks he had set aside and rubbed them together forcefully. "Act like one of the sticks is a vegetable peeler and the other is a carrot. And before you know it"—he continued to rub the sticks together

50

for about thirty seconds, then a spark suddenly appeared—"you've got fire."

"C'mon, baby, light my fire," Tyson sang off-key as Wes ignited the kindling.

"Now, as the fire gets bigger," Wes instructed, "you want to lay larger pieces of dry wood over the top of your structure, making sure there's enough room between the pieces for air to get in. Let's look for those now and set them aside."

As we walked off in all directions to collect the wood the fire continued to grow and grow. Everything was bathed in firelight—the scene was beautiful.

"Okay, put the wood over here and find some rocks to place around the fire," Wes called. "This will set our parameters and prevent it from spreading."

Once we'd formed a circle of rocks around the fire, Wes told us to gather sticks for cooking. These would be our spears for our buns, hot dogs, and marshmallows.

"Appetizer, entrée, and dessert," Stephanie quipped, probably thinking about her favorite New York restaurant. There were very few places I'd been to in Oklahoma City where you could have an appetizer, entrée, and dessert unless you counted McDonald's french fries, Big Mac, and apple pie. So this hot dog and marshmallow meal suited me fine.

"Many campers bring along a stove these days, but since we're survivalists, we're going to do this the old-fashioned way: Char it," Wes said after we'd all selected our spears. "Let's all sit outside the rocks around our fire. Then hand over the food, please."

I sat down between Steph and Betty alongside the crackling inferno. I opened my day pack to retrieve the paper plates. "Do plates count as food as well?" I joked.

"I'm so hungry I *could* eat a plate," Ryan said. "That thunder you thought you heard a couple of minutes ago? That was just my stomach growling."

Everyone—myself included—laughed. I hated to chuckle at someone I hated so much, but I had noticed over the years that Ryan *could* be funny, when he wasn't being a jerk. But that wasn't too often.

"What would've happened if it did downpour when we were building that fire?" asked Betty as she speared a beef hot dog and placed it in the flames.

"It would've been quite tough," Wes said quickly, "but not impossible. We'd crisscross some twigs on the wet ground and place our tinder on top of them. Then we would've used a large amount of tree bark as kindling. We'd have to try to block the fire as much as possible from wind with our bodies or belongings, and we'd have to use matches since rubbing two wet sticks together to create a fire in a downpour isn't exactly the most fun thing in the world to do."

"You know so much about this stuff," Stephanie said, taking a bite of her veggie dog.

I bit into my turkey dog—it was delicious. Cooked to perfection. "How long have you been doing these trips?" I asked.

"A little over five years," Wes answered, cooking his dog to a crisp in the open flames. "I actually took a survival trip, just like you guys, senior year of high school. After that I was pretty much hooked. I hope to start my own company someday."

Taking a deep breath of the woodsy air, alive with the smells of our campfire, I envied Wes's job and his lifestyle. This was living, no doubt about it.

"That's awesome," Daisy commented between bites. "What was your major?"

"Environmental studies," he said, mouth full. "And the owner of Adventure Trails, who's out with the Extreme Group now, graduated with the same degree from my alma mater a few years before I did. So it worked out pretty nicely." He scanned our faces around the campfire. "How about you guys? What do you want to be? Let's go around the circle. Steph, you first."

"I want to be a buyer," she said. "As in, you know, clothes. For department stores."

Then all eyes were on me, and I realized it was my turn. "PE teacher," I said, taking a break from my half-eaten turkey dog. It's what I'd wanted to be since sixth grade, when I'd had a former Dallas Cowboys cheerleader named Mrs. Lincoln for PE. She was awesome and dynamic and had given me real appreciation for fitness and athletics. I wanted to have that kind of impact on kids.

Betty was next. "I want to be a professional snowboarder," she said with conviction.

"I want to be a business executive," Dirk told us, smiling. "Just like my father."

Hmmm, I thought, my eyes lingering on him. So we didn't exactly share the same hopes and goals for the future. I found the business world as exciting as my chemistry textbook. *But we could work through that,* I thought, *opposites attract*—

Just then Daisy's response, "happy," yanked me from my daydreams. What the heck was a *happy?* Then I realized that she had the classic crunchy granola response. It was kind of cool too, when you thought about it. She didn't want to be anything specific in the future, she just wanted to be happy. That was a goal we all should strive for. It was something for me to remember too, what with Ryan here and all, sitting just a few feet away, directly across from me. I glanced over at him to find him staring straight at me. He looked away quickly, and I held myself back from getting worked up all over again.

"I want to be a forest ranger," Tyson said. With his stocky frame and strawberry blond hair, he actually looked like a lumberjack. Kind of like the guy on the Brawny paper towel commercials, only shorter.

Ryan's turn was next. I couldn't wait to hear this one—president of the United States, no doubt.

He hesitated a moment. "Um, I want to be a photographer."

My eyes widened in surprise. A photographer? Ryan wasn't on the yearbook or newspaper staff or anything. Maybe he'd just wanted to sound artsy and interesting in front of the group. My eyes rested on him for a moment, trying to determine if he was telling the truth. But he was just gazing into the fire, his expression not giving anything away. Well, in any case, I knew his true colors.

"It sounds like you're all going to be shooting stars," Wes declared. "Since it looks like everyone's already wolfed down the hot dogs, I propose a marsh-mallow toast."

Daisy removed the jumbo marshmallows from her pack and divvied them up among us all.

"Okay, here's how we do it," Wes began. "Spear your marshmallows in preparation, and when I say 'cheers,' we clink them in the middle of the fire. Got it?"

We all nodded, and I noticed how haunted and ro-mantic everyone looked in the firelight under the star-filled sky. The fiery glow made everyone—especially Dirk and except Ryan—look gorgeous and surreal. I smiled to myself, thinking that if this beauty tip were more publicized, millions of people would forgo plas-tic surgery and get fireplaces instead.

"Here's to seventeen more days of ultimate adventure, roaring campfires, and love for your fellow camper," Wes announced. "Cheers!"

"Cheers," we repeated in unison, clinking our

marshmallows in the center of the fire.

Ultimate adventure, roaring campfires, and love for your fellow camper, huh? I thought as I blew on my marshmallow to cool it off. I glanced over at Ryan, who was chewing away. Well, two out of three wasn't bad.

"These beds aren't too uncomfortable," I whispered to Steph a few hours later, right after we'd tucked ourselves in. "I thought they'd be stiff as a board."

"Yeah, they're kind of like my futon back home," Steph said. "Are these what your beds in camp were like?"

"Oh, those were the worst," I told her. "But when you're in sixth grade, comfort isn't your main concern."

"Mmm," Steph responded. "And given your interest in Dirk, it seems it isn't your main concern in twelfth grade either."

I laughed. "Yeah, I definitely have boys on the brain." I turned onto my stomach. "So, you come to your senses about Ryan yet?"

"I still think he's completely cute," she admitted.

"More like completely conceited," I told her, cringing at the thought that someone could actually be interested in Ryan. "But you'll find out for yourself soon enough."

"We'll see about that," Steph said. "How's it going with Dirk?"

I paused, mentally reviewing the day's Dirk encounters. "Okay, I guess. We had a couple of cool interactions. Although I didn't get to talk to him too much at the campfire."

She was silent for a moment. The crickets outside suddenly sounded really loud. "Don't worry—tonight was just a meet and greet," she said. "Tomorrow we'll start going in for the kill."

I smiled. "Sounds like a plan to me."

I closed my eyes, preparing to have wonderful dreams of Dirk and romantic, Ryan-free campfires. In my dreams, at least, I could escape my enemy. In my dreams he could vanish without a trace.

Five

"IT'S TOO EARLY to even open your eyes at this hour, much less climb a rope," Stephanie growled at 7 A.M. the following morning. We were all sitting at the bottom of a bluff, killing time, while Wes secured the top ropes in preparation for our rock-climbing lesson. Steph was not pleased.

Waking Stephanie up at 5:45 had been near impossible. When I'd finally managed to drag her out of the cabin and into the main lodge, she'd whined throughout our entire breakfast of cornflakes and fruit.

"What's the matter, Steph? You're not an early riser?" Ryan asked, poking her side.

"No, and I'm not a fan of being tickled either," she said, shooting him a go-to-heck look. "I want my Starbucks."

"Miss Stephanie, the only Starbucks we have around here is the stars in the sky and the bucks in the field," Dirk commented. Even this early in the morning he looked so amazing in his faded blue T-shirt, which accentuated his blue eyes, that I was trying my hardest not to stare.

"Am I hearing moans and groans on the first full day of the trip?" Wes called as he headed down to us after having fastened the top ropes on the bluff. "This can't be."

"Coffee," Stephanie pleaded, her eyes still only half open.

"No coffee, but there's hot chocolate and tea," Wes said, removing two silver thermoses from his backpack.

"No coffee?" Steph repeated. "Who doesn't drink coffee?"

Wes smiled. "Who wants tea?"

Stephanie and Ryan raised their hands.

"Hot chocolate?" Wes asked after pouring out their tea.

Once Daisy, Tyson, and I got our liquid refreshment, Wes told us to sit down in a semicircle. "Today we're going to learn about rocks. Not pet rocks. Not Pop Rocks. Not Chris Rock. But the kind you climb. And we're going to learn how to climb them."

I was so psyched to learn about rock climbing that the ninety-minute lecture went by surprisingly quickly. Wes gave us the lowdown on rock-climbing equipment, what kind of knots you needed to know how to tie, and how to boulder. "Any questions?" he asked at the end of his speech, looking around the group.

"How do you get down after you climb up?" Tyson asked.

"You can either hike down, rappel, or lower yourself," Wes responded. "Today we're going to hike. Sound good?"

Everyone nodded.

"Okay," Wes said, "unless someone else has a question, we're going to pair off and apply what we've learned today. To make it easy, I'm going to team you up alphabetically by last name." He looked down at a sheet of paper. "It'll be Kylie and Ryan, Dirk and Stephanie, and Daisy, Tyson, and Betty—you'll have to be a threesome this morning."

"Great," I muttered under my breath. It was bad enough that last year I'd had to endure five classes with the guy taught by teachers who also favored the alphabetical system, ensuring that I'd always have a seat right next to Mr. Obnoxious. Now I had to go through it again?

Everyone walked over to meet their respective partners, but I didn't even stand up. I didn't move a muscle. Maybe if I didn't go over to him, I wouldn't really have to be his partner.

"Guess you're stuck with me, Brennan," Ryan said, standing above me.

I glanced up at him. There he was—half smile and all. Yup, there was no getting out of it. "Looks that way," I said, rolling my eyes as I rose to my feet.

"Okay, everybody, what we're going to do is

called top roping, which means a rope from the top of the climb will be holding you so you don't have to worry about hurting yourself if you slip. Your partner will serve as the belayer, securing the rope below as you climb up. He or she will shout encouragement and serve as your spotter. I've secured four ropes so at least one person from each team can go at once. Since there's an odd number of people, one person will have to do double spotting for the first group. But I must stress this is not a race—go at your own pace. When you get to the top, I'll be up there to help you untie yourself and show you the path to hike down. Then your partner will follow suit. Sound good?"

Everyone cheered, psyched to get started.

"Okay," he continued, "figure out which partner is going to go first. I'll help harness you in, then I'll head to the top of the cliff. As soon as I'm up there and I give the go-ahead you'll start climbing. Any questions?"

"Let's get going!" Betty exclaimed.

"All right, then," Wes said. "Get prepared to climb."

Despite the fact that I was bummed to be paired with Ryan, I was still very excited to rock climb. "I want to go first," I told Ryan.

"Okay," he said, shrugging. I was surprised it was that easy. I was waiting for his smart-guy remark. But he didn't say anything more.

I looked over at Steph and saw that Wes was helping her to get ready. "You going first?" I asked.

She nodded slowly, looking positively terrified.

I tilted my head and sized up the bluff. It was only about forty feet high, but since I'd never rock climbed before, I had to admit that it looked fairly intimidating. My heart began to race as Wes walked over and helped me get harnessed in.

"You okay?" he asked.

"I think so," I said, thankful for the cool morning breeze. If it hadn't been blowing, I would have been sweating like crazy.

"Nervous, Brennan?" Ryan said as Wes walked away.

"No, not at all," I said, trying to sound confident. If he knew I felt uneasy, I'd never hear the end of it.

"Okay, looks like everyone's roped in," Wes called.

I glanced around at the group. Stephanie, Tyson, Betty, and I were all strapped and ready to go. My pulse quickened even more.

"I'm going to head up the cliff. Then we're off," Wes told us.

As Wes jogged away I looked over to Stephanie. "Steph, are you doing all right?" I asked. "You look like you're totally stressing."

"I think it'll be okay." She smiled, but it didn't conceal her fright. "Just like going up the escalator at Macy's. Only there's no escalator. And Macy's doesn't go up this high."

"You'll do fine," Ryan piped up from behind me.

Maybe he's interested in Steph, I thought. *After all, words of encouragement are rare for him.*

"You're going to be amazing, Steph," Dirk said, running his fingers through his sandy hair.

"And it's a beautiful day," I added, breathing in the fresh air. Trying to make Steph feel better took my mind off my own nervousness.

"I'll take my Manhattan pollution any day," Stephanie whined crankily, then laughed. "I know I'm being a complete baby. But humor me."

Dirk poked her on the arm. "None of that nonsense, little lady. You get happy or get out!"

Our chuckles were interrupted by Wes's bellowing from the top of the bluff. We looked up to see him beaming down on us. "Okay, guys, feeling good?"

We cheered like members of a pom-pom squad.

"I didn't hear you," Wes teased. "Are we *feeling good?*"

Our hoots and hollers echoed through the crisp air as we got into position. My heart was pumping with a combination of fear and excitement.

"Don't worry, Brennan," Ryan said from behind me. "I'll be an awesome spotter. When you slip, I'll be here to catch you."

I turned around and saw the familiar amused expression in Ryan's light blue eyes. "Don't *you* worry," I told him, "'cause I'm not going to slip." Now I'd forgotten my fears. Fueled by anger toward Ryan, I was determined to go for the gusto, give it all I had.

"Any last-minute questions, concerns, or worries?" Wes called down. When his question was met with silence, he gave us the go-ahead. "On your mark, get set, go!"

I took a deep breath and started to climb with a surge of enthusiasm. Per Wes's suggestion, I didn't look down or to either side, only straight up. I concentrated on the blue sky and cottonlike clouds above. It almost looked like I was climbing right up into the sky. I loved the feeling of the rush of adrenaline that was coursing through my blood.

I could hear Ryan shout, "You go, Kylie!" as I climbed higher and higher. I was slightly surprised by Ryan's positive shouts, but I smiled as I realized that it was mostly my hatred for him that was driving me. I supposed that was some sort of reverse encouragement. Before I knew it, I had made it to the top and was being pulled up by Wes.

"Congratulations," he said, and I felt a euphoric rush as I noticed that I was the first one to make it. I had even beaten Betty! Now on solid ground, I looked down and felt a surge of pride as I saw how high up we were. Tyson and Betty were almost to the top, but Stephanie was still struggling a bit. Ryan was smiling up to me and cheering wildly. He probably thought it was his great spotting ability, rather than any skill of mine, that had caused me to climb so fast.

Wes pointed out the trail to the bottom to me, and I began to run down it. I was so exhilarated that the few minutes it took for me to get down felt like seconds.

When I reached the bottom, Ryan gave me a high five. "You were awesome, Brennan!"

"Thanks," I said, slightly blushing and taken aback by his enthusiasm. I decided not to mention how I used my dislike of him as inspiration. Instead I shifted my gaze to Dirk, who was busy cheering Stephanie. She had just reached the top. "Yay, Steph!" I called up to her, excitement still running through my veins.

I turned to Ryan. "Ready to climb?" I asked.

"Completely," he said, flashing me a full-fledged smile. "Was it incredible?"

"Yes!" I exclaimed, trying to hold on to the intense feeling I'd had as I'd scaled the bluff. "I felt like Batman." I laughed.

He laughed along with me. "Well, you performed like Batman too. I hope I do as well as you did."

I blinked back at him. What? Was Ryan Baron actually being humble? Maybe there was a cool side to him after all; maybe—

"But then again," he continued, breaking my thoughts, "I'm sure I'll have no problem kicking your butt."

I rolled my eyes. There was the Ryan Baron I knew. His nice guy act was just that—an act.

"Whatever," I said. "We'll see how you do." Then I turned my back on Ryan, prepared to ignore him until it was his turn to climb.

"Wasn't it awesome?" Betty exclaimed, running over to me with Tyson in tow.

"A total rush," I agreed.

Steph came down the trail with Wes. "I did it! I did it!" she cried out, jumping up and down.

I ran over and gave her a hug. "I'm so proud of you!" I told her. "You conquered your fear!"

"Maybe, but you were the real rock woman," she said, beaming.

"Okay, guys, ready for round two?" Wes asked us.

Ryan hooted enthusiastically. I just knew he couldn't wait to show me up.

But after Wes harnessed us and Ryan started to climb the rock face, I got my revenge. Instead of cheering for Ryan, I remained silent. He still beat out Dirk and Daisy anyway, but *I* knew that *he* knew I didn't cheer for him. And I didn't feel bad about it. Not one single bit.

"Rock climbing was awesome," Steph commented thirty minutes later on our postclimb hike to Clover Hill, which Wes said was about two miles from the bluff we'd just scaled. "Even though I was scared at first, that was so much fun!"

"It was the best," I said.

"Too bad you got Ryan as your partner and I got Dirk," Steph whispered as we trailed behind the rest of the group. "It should've been the other way around."

"No kidding." I rolled my eyes. I was pleased with how I'd handled Ryan in the end, but I was definitely relieved that my turn of pairing up with him was over. "I still don't understand what you see in him. He's just so . . . so . . ." My voice trailed off as I found myself at a loss for words.

"So, what?" Steph asked.

"I don't even know," I told her, shaking my head. "He just gets to me, that's all."

Steph smiled. "Well, that much is obvious."

"What are we going to do when we get to Clover Hill?" I heard Betty call ahead to Wes.

"Concentrate more on the adventure and less on the destination," Wes advised. "Look around. You're hiking in beautiful country here. Take it all in. Pay attention to detail."

"What kind of detail?" Tyson asked. "There's so much to see."

I looked around and wiped my brow, a bit winded from the rising heat. There *was* a lot to see—beautiful mountains, rolling hills, towering trees, blooming flowers, endless fields. It was like we had entered a paradise of sorts and the real world no longer existed.

"I know it can be overwhelming," Wes said. He turned and began to walk backward so that he could talk to us as we hiked. "But this is actually a good segue into what I wanted to talk to you guys about on the way to Clover Hill. Wildlife photography."

"All right!" Ryan said, clapping.

"I see we have one fan," Wes said. "But even if you're not shutterbugs at heart, learning about wildlife photography can open up your eyes to things you might not otherwise notice."

Wes stopped for a second and pointed to a leaf. "For instance, check out this foliage." We all gathered around him. "See the complex veins? The moist dew sprinkling its surface? The ladybug crawling on the vine? These are details that would be excellent to focus in on for a wildlife shot. And they're also things you might overlook if you're not seeing things with a photographer's eye."

Ryan removed an expensive-looking camera from his day pack. "May I?" he asked, nodding toward the leaf Wes was describing.

"Of course," Wes said. "Glad to see someone's come prepared."

"Like I said, I do want to be a photographer someday," Ryan explained. He smiled, but it was different from his usual smirk. He actually looked *shy* somehow. "Preferably for *National Geographic*," he added, polishing off his lens.

"Whoa," Wes said. "You aim high. Good for you."

Ryan's face disappeared behind his camera as he zoomed in on the shot. We all stood around him, observing. "What shutter speed would you suggest?" Ryan asked Wes.

Ryan really *was* into this whole photography thing—shutter speeds, *National Geographic*—he sounded legit.

I watched him carefully as he adjusted the camera lens, zooming in and out. He was concentrating seriously, bending down and taking a step back to get a better angle. For a split second I forgot that this was the Ryan Baron who I'd hated all these years. Somehow he suddenly seemed like a new person to me. I found myself wondering how things looked through that lens. *Maybe he could teach me about photography,* I thought.

"What are you staring at, Ky?" Steph teased, nudging me. "Never seen a guy take a picture before?"

"Huh?" I blushed. Why *was* I staring? "Oh, uh, I guess I spaced out," I said finally, trying to snap out of it.

"Okay, guys," Wes called. "Let's get moving again. But Ryan—or anyone—if you want to stop again for a photo opportunity, just give a holler." Wes began to walk, and we all followed him like before. "And just so you all know," he called over his shoulder, "we're going mountain biking when we get to Clover Hill."

The whole group cheered and clapped enthusiastically.

"So, what were you thinking about before?" Steph asked a moment later, hiking next to me.

"When?"

Steph rolled her eyes. "Just now, when Ryan stopped to take a photo."

"Oh. Dirk," I fibbed, confused.

"Of course; I should've known," Steph said. "That clears it all up."

But as we hiked along the sun-dappled trail my thoughts were anything but clear. Why had I just lied to my best camp bud? And why was I thinking

69

about Ryan instead of Dirk in the first place? I didn't care if he could take a picture or not. And just because there was one little thing about him that I hadn't known, that didn't mean he wasn't still a complete and total jerk.

Steph gave me a long sideways glance as we hiked up a steep hill. "You okay, Ky? You look a little weird."

"I'm fine," I said, plastering a grin on my face. "Just fine."

Six

THE NEXT MORNING I awoke with a start to the sound of a loud knock. "Rise and shine, girls!" Wes hollered through the wooden door. "Breakfast's in twenty minutes."

Squinting wearily, I focused on my watch. It was 7:15. Steph and I must have stayed up too late talking last night. Either that or the rock climbing had really taken its toll because I didn't want to get out of bed, and that was totally unlike me. Usually I was an easy riser, especially when I had something to look forward to. I glanced over to Steph. It didn't look like she was in much better shape than I was. There was no sign of life whatsoever from her bed.

I closed my eyes for another five minutes, then forced myself to wake up. "Hey, Steph, move it," I said as I stood, slightly shaking her lifeless form. "Breakfast is in twenty."

I heard a small groan from under the covers. At

least I knew she was alive. "C'mon, Steph, time to get up," I said, shaking her once again. But she didn't move.

I abandoned hope and began to get ready. After taking a quick shower without hot water, I was feeling a lot more awake.

I walked over to my pile of clothes and considered what I could possibly wear that didn't look like I was trying to make an effort but would make me look good—I was still trying to catch Dirk's attention. I didn't get to talk with him much yesterday, and I was determined that today was the day to make serious progress.

After careful deliberation I decided to put on a white T-shirt, denim shorts, and hiking boots. To complete the look, I put my damp hair into two braids and coated my lips with a clear gloss.

Then I tried to wake Steph again. "Girl, you gotta get up." No response. "Listen, I'm going to look way cuter than you, and you wouldn't want that, right?"

My comment had the effect I was hoping for— Stephanie's head immediately poked out from under the covers. "Oh, you do look cute," she said, giving me a sleepy look. "What should I wear?"

"I don't know, but breakfast's in ten minutes," I told her, glancing down at my watch. "If you want to take a shower, you better get a move on."

This sent Steph into action. She jumped up, then looked over at me pleadingly. "Don't leave without me, 'kay?" she said.

I nodded, figuring I could use the time to write a couple of quick postcards to my family and Jenni.

I sat down on my bed, grabbed a pen and two of the Adventure Trails postcards Wes had given us the first day, and began.

Dear Mom, Dad, and Matty,

Having a blast in Colorado. So far we've gone hiking, biking, and rock climbing plus had some really cool campfires. Tonight is our first overnighter to Bullseye, and I can't wait. Right now Steph and I are staying in this cabin that reminds me exactly of Wanakawa from sixth grade! Miss you.

Love,
Kylie

I decided not to mention the fact that Ryan was on the trip because I didn't want them to worry. After all, they knew how much I hated him. Next was Jenni's postcard. Hers was going to have more information since I'd include all the boy stuff. I wrote really small in order to pack all the juicy details in.

Dear Jenni,

Missing you mucho in Colorado. Guess who's here—Ryan Baron! I can't believe my bad luck. The one person I tried to get away from—he haunts me! But he hasn't managed to ruin my trip, thanks in large part to the presence of one Dirk Frazier from Texas, the hottest guy I've ever seen. Blond hair, dark tan, perfect smile. Hopefully by the next time I write, he'll be my boyfriend! How's the internship and Cool Beans?

Love you,
Kylie

Steph exited the bathroom, hair covered in a towel. "What do you think about a white V-neck baby T and black shorts?" she asked, frantic. "And I'll put my hair in a ponytail, tied with black ribbon?"

"Sounds cute to me," I told her, "as long as you make it snappy. I'm starving."

Once Stephanie was primped, we headed to the main lodge. As we entered the kitchen the delicious smells of breakfast food came wafting toward us. Everyone else was already there, beginning to cook up a big meal. Dirk—looking way cute in a green T-shirt and plaid shorts—was squeezing fresh orange juice. Ryan, who was stirring up something in a bowl, had a white chef's hat and apron on, which, I had to admit, looked pretty funny.

"Hey, guys," Wes said, "grab a spatula and get on in here. We're making a special big country breakfast this morning, and we need someone on egg patrol."

"Cool. I love to cook," I said. "Scrambled okay?" My scrambled eggs were legendary in the Brennan family.

"Sure," Wes said. "The eggs are right here, and we've got some stuff in the fridge you could use to jazz them up. Totally up to you, of course."

"Great." I stepped up to the counter by the stove, where the eggs were laid out. Steph stood right next to me, and I noticed that she had a worried look on her face. "What's wrong?" I asked her.

"Nothing," she said, her brow furrowing. "It's just that I don't really know how to cook."

"That's okay," I told her. "Leave it to me. You can be my sous-chef."

"Thanks." She smiled. "So, what do you need?"

"Let's see." I put my hands on my hips as I assessed the situation. "We need a skillet and a whisk. And you could check the fridge for milk, onion, cheese, green pepper, or anything else that you think would be good in scrambled eggs."

"Aye, aye, chef," Steph responded, walking over to the refrigerator.

I went to work cracking the eggs open in a bowl. Ryan was standing to the left of me, and I couldn't help peering over his shoulder to see what he was concocting. He might be wearing the chef's hat, but I seriously doubted he knew what he was doing in the kitchen.

"Whaddya making there?" I asked him, looking at the batter he was stirring in a bowl.

75

He glanced up at me, raising his eyebrows. "Only the best pancakes you'll ever eat, Brennan. So just sit tight."

"Oh, yeah?" I concentrated back on my bowl, cracking the last couple of eggs. "I highly doubt that since *my* chocolate chip pancakes are famous."

Ryan shook his head. "Well, these are blueberry-banana. And I'm sure they're gonna be much better than your silly scrambled eggs over there."

"Really?" I crossed my arms over my chest and moved right next to Ryan, checking out his ingredients. "Did you put any vanilla extract in that batter? Pancakes just aren't the same without it, and I don't see any."

Ryan's mouth formed into a smile as he slowly reached inside his apron pocket and pulled out a bottle of vanilla extract, waving it in my face. "There you are, Ms. Julia Child. So you just stop telling me how to make my pancakes and get started on your eggs."

"I will," I told him. "You're gonna be blown away by them too."

Steph walked over, her hands full. "Here, I think I got everything," she said, dumping the ingredients on the counter.

"Great, thanks," I said. As I whisked the eggs and told Steph what to cut up and organize Ryan began to peer over my shoulder.

"Hey, I don't see any cheese over there," he commented. "You got to have cheese in your scrambled eggs."

"We've got plenty of cheese." I pointed to the large hunk of cheddar that Steph had brought from the fridge. "Now you keep your nose out of my eggs," I said, nudging him with my elbow, "and get to work on your blueberry-banana whatever."

"I see. You can put your nose wherever you like, Brennan, but I have to watch my own," Ryan teased, stepping back to his pancakes.

I laughed. "Yes, Ryan, that's exactly it. You're finally learning."

Ryan laughed too, shaking his head. "I guess sometimes it takes me a while."

"Hey," Wes called from the doorway, "are you guys cooking or fighting in there? It's getting kind of late."

I looked around the room, wondering if Wes was talking to Ryan and me or someone else in the group. But all the others were quiet at work—Daisy was making biscuits, and Tyson and Betty looked like they were nearly done with the bacon. Dirk wasn't even in the kitchen anymore. Maybe he was busy setting the table. "We're cooking," I called to Wes.

"Yeah," Ryan said. "We'll be done in no time."

"Great." Wes walked back into the dining room.

"As long as Brennan stops bothering me," Ryan added under his breath.

"Hey!" I said, lifting my whisk as a weapon.

Ryan smiled. "You heard the man. We don't have time to be messin' around."

"Please!" I exclaimed, rolling my eyes at Steph. But annoyed as I was, I also couldn't help cracking a smile.

"I'm sure I now know everything there is to know about backpacks," I said to Steph that afternoon. We both plopped down onto my bed, our tummies filled with the grilled cheese sandwiches we'd eaten for lunch. Wes had given us his "Backpack Attack" lecture earlier that day.

"Yeah," Steph agreed. "I never realized that the way you pack your bag makes such a difference. And it was wild how much stuff Wes got into his! He had like three suitcases' worth of stuff in that bag."

"Wes is very cool," I said. "And cute too. Too bad he's not ten years younger."

"Then Dirk would have some competition, right?" She laughed.

"Yeah," I admitted. "But it's not like I'm getting him anyway. I've made completely no progress."

Steph frowned. "Not true. You guys were talking a lot when we went biking yesterday."

"But he was talking a lot to *everybody*," I said. "You think he likes Daisy?"

"No way," Steph insisted. "She's too much of a hippie girl for him."

"Maybe." I stood up and began to pace around our small cabin. "I think I need some sort of plan to get his attention. What about you and Ryan? Any progress?" I put my hands on my hips. "Or have you finally realized that boy is unlikable?"

Steph shook her head. "Nah, I still like him. But I've made negative progress as well. I think I'm running a close second to his Nikon at the moment. You saw how he was snapping photos during Wes's lecture, right?"

I nodded. "That camera thing is a total shock to me." I sat down next to her again. "So is his cooking ability. I have to admit his pancakes *were* good."

"They were yummy," Steph agreed.

I nudged her. "But my eggs were better, right?"

"Of course." Steph laughed.

"'Cause I swear to God, that boy competes with me in just about everything. And there are plenty of things that I can do better than him. He just needs to get off his ego trip; he needs to—"

"Hey," Steph interrupted, "we were talking about Ryan and *me,* remember?"

"Oh, yeah, sorry." I smiled, shrugging. "Anyway, my point is that you can do better than him. Much better."

"But he hasn't been a jerk at all," Stephanie said. "He's been really nice." She gave me a sly smile. "Although I wouldn't mind if he got even nicer."

"Yeah? How much nicer?" I asked, egging her on.

"Nice enough to give me a big old kiss underneath the stars," she said dreamily,

"All right, enough!" I said, jumping up. "That's about all I can take of romantic Ryan talk." I looked at my watch. "We better start putting our packing skills to work, or they'll leave for the overnight without us."

"Okay," Steph said. "But we're not going before we come up with a plan of attack."

"What did you have in mind?" I asked, walking over to my bag to start packing.

Stephanie was quiet for a moment, thinking. "Here's the deal," she said finally. "We park our tent right next to Ryan and Dirk's tonight. They're cabin mates, so they'll be in the same one, right?"

"Right," I said cautiously. I wasn't sure I liked where she was going with this.

"And then," she continued, "you could talk to Ryan about me and I could talk to Dirk about you."

I placed my mosquito net in my backpack, glancing at Steph warily. "What am I supposed to say to him?" I asked. I didn't like this idea at all. The last thing I wanted to do was talk to Ryan about who he liked or didn't like.

"You ask Ryan in a roundabout way if he's interested in me, without being too obvious," she explained. "And I'll do the same with Dirk. I'll ask him if he has a girlfriend back home, what he thinks about you, that type of thing."

"What he thinks about me?" I repeated. "No way. That's too embarrassing. Too fifth grade."

"So I won't name names," she conceded, standing up. "I'll just ask if he likes anyone on this trip. That way he won't know I'm talking about you."

"I guess that'll be all right," I said, zipping my backpack. "But do you want me to mention your name to Ryan?"

"Sure, just be slick about it," she said. "Ask him what he thinks of me in general."

"As long as I don't have to get into a lengthy conversation," I said, cringing. "We don't usually discuss our social lives with each other, you know. Our entire relationship is based on fighting."

Steph opened up her bag. "Well, maybe you guys have reached a whole new level," she teased.

"Yeah, right." I rolled my eyes, walking over to help her pack.

"Don't worry," she assured me. "It'll take five minutes. Tops."

"I guess I can handle that. Five minutes alone with Ryan is a small price to pay for the dirt on Dirk."

"You got that straight," Stephanie said. "And before we know it, these guys will be ours!"

I smiled at Steph as she zipped up her bag, but I couldn't help still feeling uneasy at the thought of her and Ryan together.

Oh, well, I thought, reaching for my insect re-pellant. *If she really wants Ryan, I'm certainly not going to stop her now.*

The hike to the overnight campsite was exhausting, with the late afternoon sun beating down on us, lots of uphill terrain, and thick walls of mosquitoes everywhere we turned. All of these factors caused Stephanie to get supercranky, so she told me to go ahead and quicken my pace, assuring me she was content to hang back with Daisy, who liked to go slow and take in all the surrounding beauty.

As I walked faster I neared Ryan and Dirk. *If it weren't for Ryan, this would be the perfect opportunity for me to hang out with Dirk alone,* I thought, coming up right behind them. *But I guess beggars can't be choosers.*

"Hey, Kylie," Dirk said as I walked up beside him, "you gonna hike with us for a while?"

Before I had a chance to respond, Ryan smiled and said, "That is, if you can keep up."

"Yeah, whatever," I responded, "you'll be the one out of breath."

"If you do get tired, Kylie, just say so," Dirk said. "We can slow down, no problem."

I looked back at him in confusion. *Is he serious?* I thought. *I mean, I guess he's just trying to be nice and all, but still, I can hold my own.*

Ryan cracked his half smile. "A word of advice to you, my man," he said to Dirk. "Never imply to Kylie that she can't do something."

Dirk glanced at me, looking slightly worried. "I'm sorry. I didn't mean—"

"I know," I told him. "Don't worry about it. You were being sweet."

"Sweet!" Ryan exclaimed. "If I said that, you'd kill me!"

I glared at Ryan. "Well, you and Dirk are totally different people."

Both Ryan and Dirk stared back at me. I suddenly felt extremely self-conscious. Had I just made it obvious that I liked Dirk? My cheeks flushed furiously.

Dirk grinned at me. "Yes, I guess we are."

"That's just perfect," Ryan muttered, shaking his head.

I didn't know why Ryan was making such a big deal about my comment. After all, my dislike for him was nothing new. Still, I was feeling increasingly uncomfortable as the three of us walked along in a tense silence.

I glanced over my shoulder at Steph, who was chatting happily with Daisy. They looked like they were having a lot more fun than I was. "I told Steph I'd hike with her most of the way," I told Dirk and Ryan. "I think I'll slow down and wait for her."

"Whatever pleases you." Dirk winked at me. "See you up at the campsite."

"Yeah," Ryan said.

I watched them walk ahead as I slowed my pace. That was it? I was sure Ryan was going to have some obnoxious remark for me, something about how he knew I wouldn't be able to keep up with them.

And, I realized as Steph and Daisy reached me, I felt oddly disappointed that he didn't.

Even though Stephanie and I had had no problem pitching our tent earlier that morning during our practice run, we were having a miserable time getting it assembled now. All the poles that had fit together so perfectly just hours ago made no sense to us at all anymore.

Frustrated beyond belief, I stared at the instructions for over ten minutes, but I still couldn't even begin to figure out what went where. And the wind gusts that had started to blow through weren't helping much either. Even though this was the most beautiful campsite we'd set foot on so far—unbelievable mountain views, gorgeous lush trees, a small creek shimmering in the distance—it was fast becoming my least favorite, thanks to the evil tent of ours.

Wes approached our metal-and-nylon mess. "Looks like you're having a little trouble."

"Yeah," I admitted quietly, trying to prevent Ryan from overhearing. Since Steph had insisted that we snag a spot right next to him and Dirk, they were only about five feet away. Steph, on the other hand, was more worried about her feet hurting than her pride. Right now she was too busy reapplying a Band-Aid and Neosporin to be much assistance on the tent pitching. "Can you help us?" she asked.

"Steph, we should do it ourselves," I told her.

"Great," she muttered. "Then we'll be here until September."

"Tell you what," Wes said. "Why don't you two put your heads together and see if you can come up with a solution. If you don't make any progress in five minutes or so, I'll go ahead and get you started."

I sighed and looked back down at the tent instructions. I'd already done this once already—why was I having such a hard time figuring out how to do it again?

I passed the instructions to Steph, but she was as clueless as I was. "Maybe this pole hooks into this peg," she said, unsuccessfully trying to connect the two.

"Who knows," I said. "Hand me the directions again."

As she leaned over to pass the sheet to me a gust of wind blew it right out of her hands and up high into the air. We watched in dismay as the paper disappeared into the woods.

"What are we going to do now?" Steph exclaimed.

I shook my head. "I don't know, but now we've officially littered the environment."

Ryan stuck his head out of his nearly assembled tent. "You two need a hand?" he asked, his eyes taking in our mess.

"We're perfectly capable of doing it ourselves, thank you!" I retorted.

Ryan frowned, his eyes narrowing. "Hey, I was only trying to help."

"Well, we don't need your help," I told him. "You're not the only one who can do anything around here, you know."

"Actually," Steph said slowly, giving me a pleading look, "we *do* need your help."

I stared back at Steph for a moment, trying to read her expression. And then I realized what she was trying to tell me—I'd promised to talk to Ryan about her tonight! *Oops.* In my frustration I'd spaced out on that. And Ryan wouldn't be too eager to talk to me if I continued to tell him off. I sighed. "Uh, on second thought, Ryan, we could use a hand. Thanks."

Ryan shot me a confused look. "Do you have multiple personalities or something, Sybil?"

I gave a slight laugh. "No, just major tent frustration. Sorry I lashed out at you. It's nice of you to help us out."

Ryan nodded. "No problem."

It had felt really strange to apologize to Ryan. I looked over at Steph to make sure my kindness hadn't gone unnoticed. She gave me the thumbs-up. Then she called to Dirk, who was walking over to her end of the tent.

"Okay, what you want to do first is separate the poles in order of size," Ryan said.

I had to bite my lip to stop myself from commenting on his superior attitude. I hated taking orders from him. "Yeah," I said, "I couldn't remember how I'd assembled it this morning. And then the directions went flying . . ."

"Uh-huh." Ryan motioned to Dirk. "You wanna help Steph run these main poles through the nylon hoops so they crisscross?" he called. "We'll start tensioning them into the pegs at the corners."

"Will do," Dirk called back.

Then all of a sudden I saw where I'd gone wrong. I was trying to put the wrong-size poles in the base of the tent, which had messed everything up. "Now I see what I did," I said, kicking myself. I was paying for my stupidity by having to rely on Ryan to help me.

"No biggie," Ryan said, wiping his brow. "When I was practicing at home, I had to put mine together like ten times to get it right."

What was this? The incredible Ryan was admitting

he couldn't do something right on the first try? Somebody call Ripley's.

Then I remembered that the whole point of this was supposed to be for me to find out how he felt about Steph. Now was my chance—she and Dirk were out of earshot. I stared down at the ground. *Oh, I so don't want to do this,* I thought.

I glanced up at him. "So, you having fun so far?" I asked in my best nonchalant voice.

"Fun?" Ryan repeated. "Uh, yeah, I guess."

Ryan looked just as weirded out as I was at my attempt to have a normal conversation. "Me too," I said lamely. "I love it out here."

"It's really beautiful," Ryan remarked.

Was this possibly the most uncomfortable conversation in the history of the world? I knew I had to just suck it up and get it over with.

"So," I began slowly, "what do you think about Steph?"

"Steph?" Looking perplexed, he crossed his arms over his chest. Then he glanced over at her and Dirk. "What about her?"

"Um, do you like her?" I replied, trying to sound casual.

His cheeks became a little pink. "Sure," he said. "She's cool."

This wasn't going according to plan. I couldn't tell if he *liked her* liked her or just liked her as a friend.

"You think she's totally cool or just sorta cool?" I asked, trying to ignore the sick feeling in the pit of my stomach as I heard myself sound like a total idiot. Ryan was staring back at me now—I felt like his blue eyes were piercing mine. I was beyond uncomfortable. But why should I care if I sounded dumb to Ryan? This whole conversation was making me mental.

His eyes shifted to the ground. "Totally cool, I guess," he replied. "Is she single?"

"Yeah, we single girls need to stick together," I said. I instantly felt stupid. What on earth had possessed me to make that lame statement?

Ryan's mouth formed into that famous half smile. "How could someone as cute and as cool as you be single?" He laughed.

Now I was blushing beyond control. Was he being serious or sarcastic? *Sarcastic, of course,* I thought. "Ha-ha," I said quickly, to show him I knew he was joking. "Where do we need to put those pegs?"

"Way to change the subject," Ryan said, then proceeded to point out where the pegs went.

I nodded, deciding to concentrate on the tent and nothing else. Now that I'd held up my end of the bargain with Steph, trying to talk to Ryan Baron was a thing of the past.

The minute Dirk and Ryan finished helping us assemble our tent and disappeared into their own, Steph pulled me inside.

"Okay," she whispered. "What'd he say?"

"Ryan?" I asked in an equally hushed tone.

"Yes," she said, exasperated. "Of course Ryan! Who else?"

"Well, he said he thought you were cool."

"Cool? What else?"

I pulled my knees up to my chest, trying to recall what he'd said. I didn't know if it was because I still didn't like the idea of Steph hooking up with my enemy or what, but I was feeling pretty weird about the whole situation. "He said he liked you."

Her eyes widened as big as saucers. "*Like* like? Or as a friend?"

I bit my lip. "I'm not sure," I told her hesitantly, "but he did ask if you were single."

She smiled brightly. "Yay! He must like me as more than a friend then, or why would he care if I was single?"

I nodded, my stomach twisting in circles. I didn't like this at all. "That's what I was thinking," I said.

"Cool." Steph twirled a strand of her red hair around her finger. "Well, Dirk said he thought you were cute."

I grinned. "He did? Really?"

"Yup," she said. "And he said he thought you were a sweetheart."

"A sweetheart!" Maybe this plan wasn't a bad idea. "What else?"

"Not much, since you didn't want me to be obvious," she said. "But I did find out he doesn't have a girlfriend back home. The coast is clear."

"That's good to know," I said.

"See," Steph remarked happily, "before we know it, those two will be ours."

"You may be right." I lay back in the tent for a moment to get a quick rest in before dinner. As I stared up at the nylon ceiling I ignored the strange feelings I had about Steph and Ryan getting together and instead tried to focus on my Dirk fantasies. After all, he was the one I'd wanted all along, wasn't he?

An hour and a half later we were all gathered around a roaring campfire. It had cooled off considerably—the night was clear and crisp, which was refreshing. The campsite was spectacular in the daylight because of the surrounding mountains, but the darkness gave the setting a different kind of coziness. The smells of the crackling fire filled my lungs as I was once again overcome by the beauty of the dark sky, blanketed with stars. It was like sensory overload. And with Dirk sitting right beside me, who knew where this night would take us?

Wes pulled me out of my dreamy haze by suggesting that we all play a game.

"What kind of game?" Betty asked.

"It's called I'm going on a picnic," Wes explained. "The first person says what they're going to bring for a picnic, and then the second person has to repeat what the first person said plus a new item. Then the next person has to repeat what the previous people said plus whatever they're bringing, and so on and so forth. Got it?"

"My brother loves that game," I said. "Although he is in fifth grade."

Everyone laughed.

"C'mon, it'll be fun," Wes said. "I promise."

Everyone agreed to play, but I would've preferred to talk to Dirk for a while instead. We hadn't really said that much to each other during dinner. I wondered if I was supposed to make a move on him or just let things progress naturally. So far I'd chosen the latter, but nothing really seemed to be happening between us yet.

"Okay, Kylie," Wes said, "since you've played this before, why don't you go first?"

"All right," I said. "Um, I'm going on a picnic, and I'm bringing . . . my killer scrambled eggs."

Ryan laughed, and I glanced over at him. He was sitting across from me, saying something to Steph, who was right by his side. I watched them interact for a moment, wondering how they were getting along. They seemed to be smiling at each other a lot.

"Dirk, you're next," Wes said. "We'll just go around the circle clockwise."

"What do I do again?" he asked.

"Repeat what I said and add your own item," I explained.

"Okay." He winked at me. "I'm going on a picnic, and I'm bringing Kylie's killer scrambled eggs and turkey burgers."

Daisy was next. "I'm going on a picnic, and I'm bringing Kylie's killer scrambled eggs, turkey burgers, and tofu salad."

Tyson took a deep breath. "I'm going on a picnic,

and I'm bringing Kylie's killer scrambled eggs, turkey burgers, uh, tofu salad, and . . . hot dogs."

"All righty." Betty laughed, swatting a mosquito on her neck. "I'm going on a picnic, and I'm bringing Kylie's killer scrambled eggs . . . turkey burgers, tofu salad, um, hot dogs, and macaroni and cheese."

"Let's see," Wes began, "I'm going on a picnic, and I'm bringing Kylie's killer scrambled eggs, turkey burgers, tofu salad, hot dogs, macaroni and cheese, and fish sticks."

"Whoa—you're good." Ryan chuckled, firelight flickering over his features. "Okay, I'm going on a picnic, and I'm bringing Kylie's killer scrambled eggs, turkey burgers, tofu salad, hot dogs, macaroni and cheese, fish sticks, and . . . my better-than-Kylie's-killer-scrambled-eggs blueberry-banana pancakes." He looked over at me, that half smile forming on his lips.

"You wish, Ryan," I said. "My eggs kicked your pancakes' butt."

"Yeah?" Ryan's eyes lit up. "We could take a little poll among the group. Whaddya say?"

I smiled. "I'm game."

"C'mon, guys," Wes broke in. "We're not having any competitions here. This trip is about teamwork, remember?"

"Yeah," Tyson agreed. "Besides, we have to finish this exciting picnic game."

"Hey, don't go raggin' on the game, now," Wes teased.

"I was kidding anyway," Ryan said. He grinned

at me. "Brennan, your eggs weren't that bad."

"Wow, that's a big thing for you to admit," I teased, locking eyes with him. "Your pancakes weren't horrible either."

"I'm glad to see this reconciliation," Wes said. "And for the record, I thought both the eggs and the pancakes were darn good."

"I agree," Daisy put in. "Now, should we get on with the game?"

"Certainly," Wes said. "Steph, I do believe it's your turn."

"No fair!" Steph complained. "How am I supposed to remember?"

"Just try," Betty said. "It's probably easier than you think."

"All right, but my memory is the worst. Here goes. I'm going on a picnic, and I'm bringing Kylie's killer scrambled eggs . . . tof—I mean, turkey burgers . . . tofu salad . . . hot dogs, mac and cheese . . . fish sticks, Ryan's better-than-Kylie's-killer-scrambled-eggs blueberry-banana pancakes, and . . . paper plates." We all looked at her quizzically. "I told you, I don't cook."

Everyone laughed. The game continued to heat up until we were up to about fourteen items. At that point the whole group started to experience memory loss. But Dirk was the first one to take the fall.

"Let me just say that I'd never come to this picnic if I had to carry all this stuff," Dirk remarked. "But I'll give it a shot. I'm going on a picnic, and I'm bringing Kylie's killer scrambled eggs, turkey burgers, tofu salad, hot dogs, mac and cheese, uh, fish sticks, Ryan's better-than-Kylie's-killer-scrambled-eggs blueberry-banana pancakes, paper plates, bean burritos, biscuits, tomato soup, lasagna, pizza rolls, tuna fish sandwiches, and . . . oh, what did you say, Baron? Something weird. Hold on a sec. What was it? Meat loaf?"

"No, pot roast," Ryan said triumphantly. "You're out."

"We're supposed to keep going until only one person is left," Wes said. "Or we could always continue the game tomorrow since y'all are starting to look pretty tired."

We took a vote, and sleep won by a large margin. Within minutes we had all gone into our respective tents, ready to collapse for the night.

Once I settled into my sleeping bag, I realized that I actually wasn't very tired. But I was psyched to sleep outside—there was nothing like camping out in the great outdoors.

"How do you think it's going with Dirk?" Steph whispered, lying next to me in her red sleeping bag.

"Not great," I admitted. "How about you and Ryan?"

"The same," Steph said. "I guess we both should give it some time."

"Yes, let's," I agreed, curling up my toes at the bottom of my sleeping bag. "Only time will tell."

A few hours later I woke with a start to the loud sound of an owl hooting, followed by a chorus of chirping crickets. It sounded like a nature documentary was being played at full blast or something. Stephanie was snoozing like a baby beside me, but I didn't think I'd be able to fall back asleep.

Being as quiet as possible, I slipped on my jeans, T-shirt, and shoes, then slowly unzipped the tent and stepped outside. Looking at the stars usually made me sleepy—I hoped it would do the trick tonight.

My heart hammered at full force when I saw that Dirk—in a rumpled T-shirt and khakis—was parked outside his tent as well. "What are you doing?" I whispered, causing him to practically jump out of his skin. "Oops, I didn't mean to scare you."

He laughed. "That's okay. I just didn't expect to see anyone else out here at three A.M."

"Couldn't sleep with all that picnic stuff going through my head," I said, not quite believing my good fortune. I had the guy all to myself under a sky full of stars! I couldn't have planned this any better if I'd tried.

"Me neither," he confessed, running a finger through his blond hair. "Even though it sounds dumb, I'm actually kind of homesick."

"Really?" *Oooh! That's so cute!* I sat down beside him. "What are you homesick for?"

Dirk turned his head to look at me. Staring into his dark blue eyes sent goose bumps up my arms. "My father," he said.

"Oh. Are you guys really close?"

95

Dirk nodded. "We hang out a lot. And we do lots of cool things together."

I smiled at him. This guy was like my dream guy or something! I mean, how many teenage guys really had an appreciation for their family? "What kinds of things?"

"Well, our favorite activity is hunting," he told me.

What? My jaw dropped to the ground. "Hunting!" I exclaimed.

Dirk smiled playfully. "Let me guess—you're against hunting."

"Of course!" I responded. "Why would you want to kill innocent animals?"

"Don't knock it until you've tried it."

"No thanks." I shook my head. "I will never hunt. And I can't believe that you do."

"I have a question for you, then. Do you wear leather?" Dirk asked.

"Well, yes," I responded, "but—"

"But nothing," Dirk interrupted. "Leather comes from cows. Someone killed a cow for your shoes. Only difference in hunting is that we kill the animals ourselves. You let someone else do it."

"No, it's completely different." I crossed my arms over my chest. "Cows are killed for their meat anyway. You like to kill cute furry animals just for the fun of it."

"Mm-hm, I see," Dirk said, nodding. "Cows aren't cute, so it's okay to kill them. But if you're cute, you should be saved."

"That's not what I meant at all!" I responded,

completely frustrated. I sighed. "I think hunting's cruel, plain and simple. You're not going to change my mind about that."

"All right." Dirk squeezed my arm. "Then why don't we agree to disagree."

I stared back at him, completely disappointed. How could this guy—my dream guy—be a hunters' advocate?

"C'mon, Kylie," he said. "Don't look at me that way. It's good to have different opinions, to argue about things. It livens things up."

He *was* right about that. I mean, I wouldn't want to go out with a guy who simply agreed with everything I said. That would be boring. "Okay. I guess that's true."

Dirk searched my face. "So you won't hold this against me?"

"I won't," I told him.

"Good," Dirk said.

But then an uncomfortable silence fell over us for the next couple of minutes. And when Dirk began to lean forward, looking as though he might go in for a kiss, I suddenly blurted, "I guess I better turn in."

Dirk stared back at me blankly. "Okay, me too," he said after a moment. "Big day tomorrow."

"Yeah." I looked at him, waiting. But waiting for what? Did I want him to kiss me or not? I didn't know. "Well, good night."

"Good night," he said.

As I entered my tent my head was a confused

blur. *I guess I better turn in.* What had possessed me to say that? I'd ruined the perfect romantic moment. And who under forty says "turn in" anyway?

But, I thought, climbing into my sleeping bag, *maybe I didn't want to kiss him after all.* He'd been right about the arguing thing—it definitely did liven things up. *But hunting?* I wasn't sure I could be into a guy who really loved to hunt.

I closed my eyes, hoping that a good night's sleep would somehow work this all out in my head. And my heart.

Seven

"OKAY, GUYS, RISE and shine," Wes bellowed
the next morning.

His voice woke me out of a strange dream.
Dirk and I were sitting together on a park bench,
but I kept looking around for someone else. I
watched all the people pass by, but I couldn't find
whoever I was looking for. I stretched my arms
above my head, wondering what that meant.

I nudged Stephanie but got no response. After I
hurriedly got dressed, I poked her again. "Time to
get up," I said cheerily. She groaned and buried her
head under her sleeping bag.

"Ryan awaits," I sang in her ear, hoping that
would spark some sign of life.

She lifted her head and opened her eyes. "What
time is it?" she whined. "Crack of dawn?"

I reached for my watch. "Nope, but close. It's
seven."

"Oh, man," she groaned, her head disappearing into the sleeping bag again.

"Breakfast in ten minutes, everyone," Wes boomed from outside. "Then it's fish time."

"You better get up," I said to the lump that Steph had formed into. I heard rustling and voices outside our tent—some of the others must be up already. I lowered my voice to a whisper and said, "Guess who I bumped into last night?"

Stephanie finally sat up. She gave me a confused look. "When last night? I was with you last night."

"After you went to sleep," I answered. "The noises outside woke me up, and I couldn't go back to sleep. So I went outside the tent and there he was, looking at the stars."

"Oh, my gosh, talk about fate!" Stephanie exclaimed. "Were you totally psyched?"

"More like shocked, actually, to see him sitting out there at three in the morning."

"So what happened?" she asked, fully awake now. "Spare no details."

"He told me about being homesick for his father, which was sweet." I gathered my hair up into a ponytail. "But then our conversation got kinda weird."

"How so?" she asked.

"Uh, he told me that he likes to hunt."

"Really?" Steph scrunched her nose up in disgust. "That's horrible."

"I know. We sort of got into a mini-argument about it."

Steph laughed. "I can imagine. So I take it there was no kissing action."

I shook my head. "Hardly."

"How did it end?"

"That whole hunting thing threw me, and then it almost looked like he was going to make a move," I told her. "So I started to panic, and out of nowhere I go, 'I guess I better turn in.'"

"Turn in?" Steph repeated, dropping her jaw.

"I know, I sounded completely lame," I said, laughing. "But I was desperate for something to say."

"And that's it?" she asked, rummaging in her backpack for some clothes.

I shrugged. "Yup."

"Do you still like him?"

I paused for a moment, trying to think if I'd figured it out. "I don't know," I told her. "I mean, he's so cute, and he's always sweet. But hunting might be too much to swallow. We just might be too different."

Steph put on a pair of shorts. "That would be a shame. I thought we were both going to find love on this trip."

"Yeah," I said, unzipping our tent. "Looks like one of us will have to fall in love for us both."

When Steph and I stepped out into the beautiful morning light of the campsite, we found everyone sitting around, eating breakfast. Almost everyone. "Where's Dirk and Ryan?" I asked, trying to sound as nonchalant as possible.

"I guess still waking up. Come and grab some

OJ and trail mix," Wes said. Then louder he yelled, "Ryan, Dirk, come and get it!"

Dirk stuck his head out of the tent. "Here I am," he said, joining the group. "Ryan'll be right out. You practically need a bullhorn to wake him up, I swear."

"Sounds like someone I know," I said, winking at Stephanie. I reached over to get a bowl of trail mix.

"Come on," she said as Wes filled her cup with some orange juice. "I'm not that bad."

At that moment Ryan emerged from the tent, wearing a fishing hat. I'd always wanted one of those. "Good morning, all," he said.

"At least Steph and Ryan sleep through the night," Wes said. He glanced at me and Dirk. "I heard a few of you up in the wee hours of the morning."

I blushed as Dirk said, "Guilty as charged. Those animal noises kept waking me up. What were they?"

"Oh, bears, coyotes—you name it."

Daisy gasped. "Really?"

Wes chuckled. "It's rare that you'll see one, but they are out there."

"Whoa." I shivered. "That would totally freak me out. I'm glad we didn't see anything."

"Well, then you should stay in your tent at night, missy," Ryan commented as he helped himself to some trail mix.

"Thanks, Dad," I retorted.

Ryan smiled. "Just looking out for you, Brennan."

"So, you guys ready to do a little fishing?" Wes asked.

"You betcha," Tyson said.

"What's the plan?" I asked, swallowing my last bites of trail mix.

"We're going to spend an hour or so learning about the different types of fish, lures, and flies, as well as casting techniques," Wes explained. "Then we'll head over to the Tarryall River to catch our dinner."

"Sounds awesome," Betty said, rubbing her hands together in anticipation.

"Can I catch and release?" asked Daisy, looking worried.

"Sure," Wes said. "That's up to you. We have veggie dogs for all you vegans so you won't go hungry. Don't do anything you don't want to do."

"Great," she said. "My fishies will be saved, at least."

"How many of you have fished before?" Wes asked. "Let's see a show of hands."

Everyone's but Stephanie's went up.

"Good," Wes said. "And don't worry, Steph, I'm going to explain all the basics."

"Good, 'cause I'm gonna need all the help I can get," Steph remarked.

"Here's the plan," Wes began. "We need to disassemble our tents and put them on our packs. Whoever didn't carry the tent yesterday, it's your turn today. Pack up your stuff, leave nothing behind—we

103

won't be coming back. Then we're going to head down to the Tarryall. I'll give a brief lecture there, and we'll start fishing. Then after we've caught a hundred fish"—the group laughed—"we head back to base camp and have our Phish feast. And that's *p-h-i-s-h,* not *f-i-s-h.*"

"Huh?" Betty asked.

"Phish, as in the greatest band in the world?" Daisy squealed.

"You got it," Wes said. "Music by *P-h-i-s-h* and *f-i-s-h* by us. How's that sound?"

"Rockin'," I said, psyched. This sounded like it was going to be the best day yet!

"And the person who catches the most fish wins a Phish CD," Wes said. "You up to the challenge?"

I smiled, looking over to Ryan. He lifted a single eyebrow as our eyes locked. I knew we were both thinking the same thing—that we would be the one to win the CD.

I definitely was up to the challenge.

An hour later we were on the Tarryall River, reels in hand. It was a sweltering hot, sunny day, and nothing felt better than being by the cool, serene water, the sunlight reflecting off its surface. This was the life.

"Okay, what you want to do is whip your rod back and forth," Wes instructed, "moving the line onto the water. This way the fish will think our flies are real—and alive."

"We just keep doing this?" Steph asked.

"That's right," Wes said. "Remember, the key here is patience. They'll come to the surface when they're hungry."

Ryan took off his shirt and tied it around his waist. I couldn't help sneaking a peek. And I had to admit, he might be a conceited jerk, but he *did* have a good body. A great one, actually.

Right at that moment Ryan caught me looking at him. Cheeks aflame, I quickly glanced away and focused on my fishing rod. I tried to cover up my reason for staring by saying, "It's no fair that the guys can take off their shirts when it's so hot out."

"Kylie, you're more than welcome to take your shirt off if you'd like," Dirk said.

The group laughed, causing my blush to deepen even more. *I better just keep my mouth shut for a while,* I thought, staring down at the shimmering water.

We all fished silently for a few moments. But Steph seemed to be having major problems. "Ryan, I lost my fly," she said. "Will you help me?"

Ryan looked up from his pole. "Whaddaya need?"

"Help me put this fly on the hook," she whined. "I can't put it on right—it won't stay."

"Shhh," Betty said. "You're scaring off all the fish."

Tyson and Dirk shushed her as well, which made Stephanie even more vocal about her unhappiness: "C'mon, guys. Someone has to help me. I don't know what I'm doing."

"Hold up, Steph," Wes said as he untangled Daisy's line. "I'll be over there in a sec."

Ryan rolled his eyes and grabbed the hook from

Stephanie's hands, fastening the fly himself. "There," he said, frustration evident in his voice.

"Thanks," Stephanie said quietly.

All of a sudden I felt a tug on my rod. "I got one! I got one!" I exclaimed. Before long I was reeling in a good-sized trout.

"Way to go," Ryan said, flashing me a thumbs-up. I smiled at him, then diverted my attention back to the fish that was flopping at the end of my line.

"Grab the fish by the lower jaw with your left hand and forefinger," Wes instructed, quickly approaching. "That will immobilize it and make it stop flopping around."

"Oh, man, I can't watch," Daisy said, covering her eyes with her hand.

I followed Wes's instructions, trying not to think about how slimy the fish felt. "Okay."

"Now push the shank with your pliers to remove the hook," he instructed, standing over me. "Be careful not to cut yourself."

I took the pliers out of my pocket with my free hand and did as Wes said, taking a deep breath. "All right, it's out."

"Very carefully put the fish on your stringer by pushing the loop under the fish's gills." Wes held up the cord adorned with metal loops that we'd secured to a large rock earlier. "We'll keep it in the water until we're ready to go."

"Okay," I said, completing the task. "Mission accomplished!"

Wes clapped lightly. "Fish number one has been

caught. Only ninety-nine more to go!"

"That was awesome," Steph told me. "Like a pro."

"Thanks," I said, baiting my hook again.

Dirk cocked his head at me. "Not that different from hunting, is it?"

I stared back at him. I guessed he sort of had a point. Still, there was no way I was ever going to approve of hunting. "We agree to disagree, remember?"

"Right." Dirk winked. "I gotcha."

Ryan glanced over at me. "You might've gotten the first fish, but I'm going to catch you, Brennan," he said.

"*You* need to worry about catching the fish, not me," I said with a smile, reeling my rod out onto the water.

"Oh, yeah?" he said, walking over to me.

"Yeah," I said. "That CD is going to be mine."

"Well, I'm going to stand right here, and we'll see which one of us catches a fish in the same exact place first."

"No way," I said, laughing. "You're cramping my style with that silly fisherman's hat of yours."

"Yeah, right, you're just afraid of the competition." He gave me a half smile. "Besides, you know you wish you had this hat yourself."

I looked up at his crumpled hat. "I could have it if I wanted it."

"Really?" he challenged, his eyes lighting up. "I'd like to see you try."

I quickly reached up to grab the hat off his head, but he pushed my arms away, causing me to lose

107

my balance and take a step backward, bumping into Steph. "That's it!" I exclaimed, putting down my rod and lightly pushing him, which caused him to go toppling into the river with a splash.

"Oh, my God!" I exclaimed, laughing hysterically as I saw Ryan's dripping wet form emerge from the water.

"You're asking for it, Brennan," Ryan warned with a smile, slowly walking out of the river, approaching me.

"Sshh!" Tyson hissed.

"C'mon, guys, you really are scaring the fish," Betty said.

But I couldn't help shrieking as Ryan neared me, dripping wet, threatening to pull me into the river.

"Kylie, Ryan, that's enough horseplay!" Wes snapped. "You're driving the fish away and ruining it for everyone else. Not to mention the fact that I don't like you guys fooling around while you're holding expensive equipment." He sighed, putting his hands on his hips. "I think you two should cool down and take five."

I blinked back at Wes in disbelief. *Take five?* Was he serious? Wasn't that what they did in like, *kindergarten?*

"Sorry, Wes," Ryan said.

"Uh, yeah, sorry," I muttered.

Wes shook his head. "Don't apologize. Why don't you just go over to the clearing back there"— he pointed over his shoulder—"and I'll come get you in a little while to rejoin the group."

He *was* serious! I looked at Ryan, but he just shrugged as if to say, What can we do?

"Sorry," Steph whispered to me, "that sucks."

"Thanks." I nodded. "But don't you worry, I'm still gonna win that CD."

Ryan laughed. "C'mon, Brennan, let's go serve our time."

A couple of minutes later Ryan and I dropped down in the middle of a beautiful, sprawling field. "I can't believe Wes got so mad," I said.

"I know," Ryan agreed. "He seemed like the type of guy who never loses his temper."

"I guess he is responsible for all of us," I reasoned, stretching out my legs. "Maybe he was worried that someone could've gotten hurt."

"Maybe." Ryan nodded. Then he smiled. "And we are pretty annoying."

"Yeah." I laughed. "Sorry about getting you wet. I didn't mean for you to fall in the river." I glanced over at his wet body, which was drying quickly in the hot sun. Feeling self-conscious that my eyes had rested on his chest just a moment too long, I quickly averted my gaze down to the ground.

"Sure, Brennan," he teased. "I believe that." Then I felt him place something damp on my head. "You wanted to wear my hat? You can have it now."

The coolness of the hat actually felt like a relief on my sweaty head. But I wasn't going to let Ryan know that. "Hey!" I said, taking off the hat. "I don't want your wet old hat." I tried to place it back on his head.

"No way," he said, pushing my arms away, "that's all yours now."

"I don't want it," I said, still trying to force the hat on his head.

"Then you shouldn't have thrown me in the river."

He tickled my armpit and I shrieked, collapsing with laughter. "No, don't!" I cried.

This only caused him to tickle me more. "So, you're ticklish, are you? Very interesting," he teased, his hands reaching out all over me.

"Stop!" I panted between giggles, trying to get ahold of myself. I fell backward, lying in the grass, as he continued to tickle.

"Not until you surrender," he joked, leaning over me. "Say you surrender."

I didn't say anything, and Ryan tickled even more furiously, under my neck this time.

Exhausted from laughing, I gave up. "All right, all right, I surrender."

Ryan stopped suddenly, his hands still near my neck. Then the weirdest thing happened: His blue eyes flashed from playful to serious, one of his hands relaxed on my neck, and he leaned in closer. It seemed like he was going to kiss me . . . and the really strange thing was, at that moment I wanted him to.

He leaned in closer and I closed my eyes, waiting in anticipation. . . .

"Hey, guys," Wes called.

Ryan jumped away and I sat up quickly, the two of us almost bumping heads.

Wes stood at the edge of the clearing. "You two ready to come back?" he bellowed.

"Uh, yeah," I called back, too embarrassed to look at Ryan. "We'll be right there."

Wes waved and walked away. I slowly stood up, my head spinning. What had just happened there? And why had I *wanted* it to happen?

Maybe I imagined the whole thing, I thought, brushing the grass off my shorts. *The idea of Ryan and me kissing is ridiculous.*

I began to walk back, Ryan trailing behind me.

"Perfect timing," I heard him mutter.

Neither Ryan nor I won the fish contest that day.

"Here's to the winner—Betty Thompson," Wes said that night over the Phish song "Tweezer" back in the dining room at the main lodge. "I propose a toast to the fishing victor of the day."

"Cheers," we said, clinking our cups of Coke together.

Ryan caught my eye from across the picnic table, and I glanced away. I'd been avoiding him ever since our near encounter on the field. Actually I'd been rather quiet all day, my mind racing with a million questions. What had happened out there? What *could have* happened? What did Ryan mean when he'd said "perfect timing"? Was he being serious and saying, *Thank God we didn't kiss?* Or was he being sarcastic and saying, *I really wanted to kiss*

111

you? And most important, had I temporarily lost my sanity, thinking I wanted to kiss Ryan Baron, the guy I'd hated for so many years?

"I'd like to congratulate all of you on a job well done," Wes said, pulling me out of my blur of thoughts. "Thirty-five fish, including the four that Daisy released, is not bad for a day's work."

Everyone cheered and chatted excitedly about the day's events. I didn't, though. I chewed on the rim of my paper cup, lost in my own world.

"Hey." Steph, who was sitting next to me, nudged me. "Are you all right?"

"Huh?"

"You've been kind of out of it."

"Oh," I said. "I'm just tired."

Steph nodded. "It has been a long day. But lots of fun too. This fish is awesome!"

I gave her a small smile, happy to see she was really getting into the spirit of the trip. "So you really enjoyed fishing, huh?"

"Actually—to my surprise—yes."

"See," Dirk said, sitting on the other side of me, "we're going to turn her into a regular Girl Scout."

"Well, I wouldn't go that far," Steph said. I laughed.

As the meal wound down, the candles on the table got lower and the music got louder.

Dirk tilted his head at me. "Wanna dance?" he asked, pointing to the floor space in the corner of the room where Daisy had been dancing around by herself for the last fifteen minutes.

I shot a quick glance at Ryan, who was talking

to Tyson. *Would Ryan care?* I wondered. Then I almost kicked myself—what was wrong with me? It was insane for me to think that anything could ever happen between me and Ryan, and it was definitely insane for me to *want* something to happen. This was *Ryan Baron,* my enemy from hell! Why should I care what he thought about me dancing with Dirk?

"Sure, why not?" I said, standing up and following him to the makeshift dance floor. It felt good to dance, to just let loose and feel the music, and after a couple of moments I'd managed to push the whole Ryan dilemma out of my mind.

That is, until he and Steph started to dance next to us. Watching them together caused my stomach to twist and turn in knots.

And when I saw Steph laugh and squeeze Ryan's shoulder, I thought I was going to throw up.

Snap out of it, Kylie! my mind screamed. *You don't want anything to do with Ryan—you hate him, remember?*

I took a deep breath and tried to smile at Dirk. As he smiled back I resolved to quit worrying about what my worst enemy was doing and instead focus all my attention on Dirk, who was supposed to be my dream guy.

If only I felt more excited about him, everything would have been perfect.

Eight

I LEFT THE fish fry after a couple more dances, tired and confused beyond belief. Steph was still at the main cabin, hanging with Ryan (which was causing me much discomfort), so I decided to write Jenni a follow-up letter to the postcard I'd sent her earlier. We were heading out to Yellowstone tomorrow, and this was the last chance to send any mail until the trip's end.

Dear Jenni,
What's up? It's day 4, and I couldn't be having more fun. Of course, I miss you majorly. How's life at Cool Beans? I can't wait to hear all about it. Lots has happened since my postcard. Actually, even though I'd been really bummed about Ryan being here, he hasn't been as bad as you'd think. We've had a few fights but no major blowouts. I

pushed him into the river today, which is a funny story. And then we had this *weird* moment, but I'll have to wait until I get home to tell you about it. I couldn't possibly explain it in a letter. And then that guy Dirk? I think he's interested in me, but I just don't feel a spark with him. I'm very confused. For once a gorgeous guy is available and seemingly into me, and I'm not interested. Maybe it has something to do with the fact that he likes to hunt, but—

Stephanie walked in at that moment, and I self-consciously stuck the letter in my bag.

"What was that?" Stephanie asked.

"Just a letter to Jenni," I said.

"Oh," Stephanie said, kicking off her shoes. "God, I haven't written any of my friends. They're gonna kill me."

"Nah." I shook my head. "Once they hear all about your newfound love for the great outdoors, they'll be too shocked to be mad."

"You're probably right." Steph giggled, collapsing onto her bed. "So, I take it the final verdict on Dirk is a no?"

"I guess," I told her, lying back on my own bed. "How did you know?"

"Because you bolted early tonight," Steph responded. "And you didn't seem to be too into dancing with him."

"Yeah. I mean he's cute and all, no doubt about

that." I stared up at the ceiling, trying to sort out my thoughts. Of course, Steph had no idea that Ryan was now wrapped up into my confusion. And I sure didn't want to tell her. "But there's no chemistry between us."

"I can totally relate."

"How so?" I asked.

"Me and Ryan," she said. "I'm over it."

I sat up straight "Over it?" I gasped, staring back at her. "I thought you were, like, in love with him."

Stephanie's eyes widened. "In love? Not quite."

"Wow," I muttered. "I can't believe it."

"Why are you so surprised?" Steph asked, looking at me curiously.

I glanced down to the wood floor. "I don't know. I just thought—I mean, you were dancing and everything. . . ." My voice trailed off. I lifted my eyes back up. "So you don't like him anymore?"

"Nope," she said. "We're too different—even for a summer fling. Him getting annoyed with me today when we were fishing pretty much sealed our fate. I need a man who can step up to the plate for me, not make me feel stupid for needing his help."

"So you're *really* over him?" I asked.

Stephanie gave me a weird look. "Why do you care so much if I'm over him, Ky?" she asked, her voice soft.

"Uh, I don't know," I replied, suddenly feeling really uncomfortable. I stood up and walked around the cabin, trying to make myself look busy. "No reason."

Stephanie started to laugh.

116

I glanced back at her. "What's so funny?"

"I knew it!" Stephanie said, bouncing up and down on her cot. "I totally knew it!"

"Knew what?"

"That's why you've been so preoccupied with beating Ryan in every activity we have," she said, "and why he's always talking about you! I *knew* there was something going on!"

My body stiffening, I froze in place. Had Ryan told her about what had happened between us that afternoon? "What?" I asked. "What are you talking about?"

"It all makes sense now," she said, nodding knowingly.

I put my hands on my hips. I didn't like this at all. "What makes sense?" I demanded.

"You like Ryan! And he likes you!"

"*What?*" I said. I felt like my knees were going to give. "I do not like Ryan!"

Stephanie laughed. "Yes, you do, Kylie."

My head swimming, I didn't respond for a moment. Then I sat down next to Steph on her bed. "I don't like Ryan," I repeated quietly, but this time I didn't even sound convincing to myself.

"Okay, okay—just bear with me for a second," she said, squeezing my hand. "You've been checking Ryan out lately, especially today on the water. And when I'm with him, you look totally uncomfortable . . . almost jealous. Why? Because you like Ryan. It's obvious."

I tried to absorb everything she was saying. "But

Ryan and I have been enemies, like, forever. I mean . . . I just don't . . . how could . . ." I shook my head, my voice trailing off, my mind blurry and confused.

"For enemies you two sure spend a lot of time talking to each other," Steph said. "You and Ryan were talking nonstop today. I mean, be honest, Ky. You guys don't really fight. You *flirt*."

I blinked back at her, struck by her words. And then I was stopped by a sudden flood of memories: how intrigued I was to discover Ryan's interest in photography, how confused I felt when he told me he thought I was cute and cool, how much fun I had fighting with him on the river, how I'd come so close to kissing him. *And the truth is,* I thought, the confusion I'd been feeling over the past couple of days clearing up, *I'd rather fight with Ryan than flirt with Dirk any day. Fighting with Ryan has become fun.*

Stephanie took one look at me and smiled in triumph. "I'm right, aren't I?" she crowed. "You *do* like Ryan!"

"Yes," I began slowly, my heartbeat quickening, my palms clamming up, "I think you're right. I think I might like Ryan."

"This is too rich!" Steph exclaimed, jumping up. "Once sworn enemies, now star-crossed lovers."

"But how can that be? How can I be in love with my worst enemy?" I uttered, still totally in shock over this revelation.

118

"Well," Stephanie said. "Close your eyes and think about what used to bother you about Ryan."

Even though I felt stupid doing it, I shut my lids lightly. At that moment I needed all the help I could get.

I thought about all the things about Ryan that used to annoy me: his know-it-all attitude, the fact that he beat me out of the election, those stupid bubble gum cigars, his ultracompetitive spirit, his conceit, his huge ego.

"Now," she continued, "think about what you like about him." All right: his passion for photography, how he respected my independence, his Ethan Hawke–like looks, the way he challenged me to be my best, his sharp wit, how he kept me on my toes, his athletic abilities, the fun times we had together when we fought . . .

"So, do the good things outweigh the bad?" she asked.

I opened my eyes and nodded.

Steph put her hands on her hips. "Then the old things that made him your enemy have now been canceled out by the new things that make you adore him," she said matter-of-factly. "Happens all the time."

"I guess you're right," I muttered, still in a daze.

"And being in a new environment might've been what caused this change between you two to happen," she continued. "After all, it's clear that you and Ryan have real chemistry."

Chemistry, I thought, our charged moment from earlier that day popping into my mind. A rush of pure excitement coursed through my veins as I realized just how much I'd wanted to kiss him in that field. Yes, I'd wanted to kiss Ryan Baron—the boy who had been my enemy for years. Then the sudden delirium I was feeling transformed into pure insecurity. "Oh, no," I moaned.

"What's wrong?" Stephanie asked, sitting down next to me again.

"What if Ryan doesn't like me back?"

"He does, trust me," Steph insisted. "He talks about you all the time—how many fish you caught, how fast you climbed the rocks, how good you are at hiking. The boy worships you."

I couldn't help a small smile from creeping onto my face. "He really said all that?"

"I swear," she said. "I should've realized this sooner, but I'd just figured since you went to school together and we were roomies, he felt like you were a safe topic. But now it's all becoming clear—he's crazy about you! Haven't you noticed how he looks at you?"

I just sat there, smiling brightly, feeling lightheaded and silly.

"Look at you!" Steph exclaimed. "There's no way you can say you don't like Ryan now. You're practically in a love trance!"

"Okay, okay." I giggled, my cheeks reddening. "So we established that I like him. Now what?"

Stephanie put her hands on my shoulders. "You've

120

got to tell him, Kylie. You can't keep your feelings to yourself—it'll drive you crazy. You gotta come clean."

I swallowed, feeling truly scared for the first time in my life. "How do I tell him that?" I asked. "All we ever do is fight—how do I tell him without looking stupid?"

"I know it's not an easy thing to say," Steph told me. "But you just have to do it. And believe me, he'll be psyched. But you better tell him ASAP because holding this in will be hazardous to your health." She stood up. "Heck, it will be hazardous to *my* health since I'll be the one who'll have to listen to you talk about him twenty-four seven."

"Steph!" I stood up and hit her with my pillow.

She smiled. "You gotta tell him," she said, looking straight into my eyes.

I let out a deep breath, considering what she was instructing me to do: to tell Ryan Baron that I, Kylie Brennan—former president of the I Hate Ryan society—now liked him. To put my heart on the line, when it might very well get stomped on like it did in the election. Make myself vulnerable to a guy who was always trying to show me up. I didn't know if I could do it.

But when I thought about Ryan's teasing light blue eyes, his playful smile, and the amount of fun we had on the river and then realized that all these images caused goose bumps to travel up my arms, I knew what I had to do.

"I'll tell him soon," I said to Steph. "As soon as I can."

*   *   *

Wes knocked on our cabin door early the next morning to announce that breakfast was in twenty minutes. But I had been lying awake for hours, electrified with a confusing mix of emotions. I was excited, weirded out, nervous, and exhilarated that I had realized my feelings for Ryan. But most of all, I was completely scared to face him. What would I say? What would I do? The mere thought of laying eyes on him, knowing that I liked him, paralyzed me with fright.

I got out of bed and stepped into the shower, giving myself a pep talk. *It's going to be all right,* I thought. *I'll see Ryan at breakfast and act totally normal, like I always have. I'll say good morning and joke about whatever comes to mind, as if nothing has changed. Then when the time is right, I'll tell him everything.*

But I was still feeling nauseous as I shook Stephanie, trying to get her to wake up.

"C'mon, Steph," I whined. "I really need you today."

Steph's head poked out from under the covers. "Wow, you really sound freaked. Are you that scared to see Ryan?"

I nodded gravely.

"You're not going to the firing squad, Kylie, you're going to see the guy you like," she said with a laugh. "There's a big difference."

"I know," I muttered. But given the way my

stomach was tossing and turning, my body obviously didn't think there was much of a difference at all.

Walking into the main lodge with Stephanie was torture. My belly was full of butterflies, and my mouth was dry as cotton. I opened the door, thinking, *Just act normal; it's no big deal.*

But my heart pounded against my chest when I saw Ryan. He was sitting at the picnic table, wearing an OU baseball cap and a white T-shirt, eating a bagel. He was the only person in the room that I could focus on.

"Hey, Kylie and Stephanie," Wes said, yanking me from my daze. "Grab a bagel and have a seat. We've got poppy, raisin, and onion."

As everyone greeted us I smiled weakly and grabbed a poppy seed bagel, even though I was quite certain I would not have the appetite to finish it. Then I sat down at the opposite end of the table from Ryan, between Daisy and Tyson. So much for my plans to talk to him and act normal. I could barely even look at the guy.

Wes was telling everyone that they needed to wear a hat of some kind. "This will keep the bugs out of your hair and the sun off your scalp," he explained. "You'd be surprised how much cooler it can make you too."

"But I'm already cool enough," Ryan said, smiling.

"We're talking cool as in temperature, Baron," Wes said. "Plus you're already wearing a hat, so I wasn't worried about you. Kylie, have you got one?"

I looked up, startled. "What?"

"A hat," Wes repeated. "Do you have one?"

"Um, sure," I said, hardly able to get the words out. This was pathetic. Now I couldn't even speak in Ryan's presence. Why had it been so much easier when I thought of him as my enemy?

"We should be at Vedauwoo in a couple of minutes," Wes said from behind the wheel of the Jeep Cherokee. "We're laying over there for the night, and then tomorrow it's off to Yellowstone."

The hat-covered group crowded into the car cheered, but I didn't bother to join in. Although miles upon miles of beautiful scenery were whizzing past me, I wasn't able to pay any attention. All my thoughts were on Ryan: what to say, how to say it, whether to look him in the eye. The fact that he was sitting directly in front of me, riding shotgun, didn't help my nerves much.

"I can't wait to explore the nontouristy parts of Yellowstone," said Dirk, who was squished beside me. "You know, the backcountry that hardly anyone ever explores."

"Me either," I told him, eager to talk about anything as long as it distracted me from my nervousness.

"You've never been to Yellowstone, have you?" Dirk asked.

"No," I said. "Have you?"

"Yup," he responded. "I'll point out the sights."

"Thanks," I said distractedly.

"Vedauwoo is right outside of Laramie," Wes

told us. "Once we get there, you'll have an opportunity to do some hiking and rock climbing."

Dirk winked at me. "You're gonna rock climb with me later, aren't you?"

I snuck a peek at Ryan, wondering if he'd come climbing with us as well. "Um, yeah, sure," I said.

Wes pulled the Jeep off into some brush. "Here we are, kiddos. Grab your stuff, pile out, and we'll be off to the campsite."

"You think the car is okay here?" Tyson asked, eyeing our desolate surroundings warily.

"Oh, sure," Wes replied. "I've left it here plenty of times. There isn't exactly a high crime rate around here."

Dirk opened the door and stepped down before me. "Here, Kylie, let me help you with your pack," he said, holding his hands out to me.

"Thanks," I said, giving him my backpack, then taking it back when I got out of the car.

Ryan, who was standing a few feet away, glanced over at me.

Okay, Kylie, I thought, *you have to say* something *to him— just speak!* "Uh, Ryan, are you psyched?" I managed to ask.

"Yeah," he said, smiling. "Ready to live off the land."

I was at a loss for what to say next. I looked down, embarrassed. My heart was beating so rapidly, I couldn't even form a sentence. I felt like a complete idiot—I had never been this tongue-tied, this vulnerable, in my entire life. I didn't like the feeling at all.

"What's the matter, Brennan?" Ryan asked. "You look weird."

"I do?" I replied, panicked.

"Yes," he said, his brow creasing. "What's going on in that head of yours?"

"Nothing," I said. "I'm, um, just ready to hike."

He gave me a strange look, but luckily Wes called for everyone's attention at that awkward moment. "Okay, gang, here's the story. We're going to hike about two miles to our campsite. From there you can either go rock climbing or hike some more—there's some really beautiful country to explore. Then we'll come back, set up our tents, and have a campfire."

"More hot dogs?" Betty asked, rubbing her belly.

"Yep," Wes said, "and we have some canned beans and tortillas if you want to make burritos."

"Olé!" Daisy exclaimed.

I was ready for this hike, hoping that it would clear my head. I wanted to come up with some sort of plan before approaching Ryan. I just didn't know how to tell him that I liked him without sounding like a fool. I mean, I hadn't exactly been smooth when I'd tried to wing it with Dirk—*Uh, I guess I better turn in* wasn't the coolest thing I could've said. Plus this was Ryan Baron I was about to lay myself on the line for. Every time I reminded myself of our past history, of our endless fights, the idea of telling him that I liked him caused another wave of nausea to wash over me.

"Okay, let's get going," Wes instructed.

126

I began to walk quickly, just a couple of steps behind Wes and a safe distance ahead of Ryan. But before I really got to savor my walk alone, Dirk caught up with me.

"You're keeping a fast pace today," Dirk remarked.

"Yeah, well, I was in the mood for a quick hike."

"Me too," Dirk said. "Mind if I join you?"

I didn't respond for a moment, thinking that I couldn't really tell Dirk to go away—that would be rude.

"Of course not," I said. *Besides,* I thought, *hopefully some mindless chitchat will help me to relax.*

Hours later I still hadn't relaxed. That evening I sat around the campfire between Dirk and Stephanie, a queasy feeling overtaking my stomach. And it wasn't due to the burritos either—Ryan was sitting across from me, looking cuter than ever as the firelight cast a glow on his features, illuminating his eyes and his smile. I couldn't look at him without getting embarrassed. But I was determined to tell him how I felt, first thing tomorrow. Steph was right—my happiness depended on it.

That afternoon I'd been a hopeless klutz rock climbing with Dirk, Wes, Steph, and Betty. When Ryan had chosen to go hiking, I'd figured that at least I'd be able to act normal during our rock climb. But I couldn't have been more wrong—my mind had been so caught up with thoughts of Ryan that I couldn't concentrate, and I kept tripping all over the place. Steph was doing a better job than I was. That's when I realized I had to talk to Ryan as soon as possible, before I ruined the trip for myself with my ridiculous behavior. Yep, I had to just swallow my pride and tell him everything.

At the moment Daisy was wrapping up a ghost story, which felt especially eerie in our isolated spot in the mountains under the dark night sky. "The cheerleaders hear a rustling outside, then a hunch-backed man's shadow begins to form on their tent," Daisy said. "Someone's out there! Then they see his hand rise up ever so slowly"—she raised her own tight-clenched fist—"and make out the shape of a sharp, pointy knife. One of the girls picks up her cell phone and frantically dials 911, but it won't work because it's out of range."

Daisy paused dramatically, and I heard Steph gasp in anticipation. "Then the door of their tent begins to unzip very slowly, and the hunchback sticks his big, burly arm in the tent. The girls scream in terror. There's nowhere to run. There's nowhere to hide. He ambushes the tent and starts slashing up the girls' wrists and necks one by one. He keeps saying, 'This is for Tina, this is for Tina,' over and over again. 'Who's Tina?' they scream, necks and arms covered with blood. 'My daughter,' he says, slashing again and again and again. 'The one you beat out for cheerleader.' The girls beg him to stop, but his knife is unforgiving. Miraculously one of the girls manages to escape while his back is turned. The next morning officials find the bodies, accompanied by a suicide note: 'We slash our necks as a symbol of all the others' throats we've cut as cheerleaders. We slash our wrists for all the pompoms we've wielded as weapons against those less popular than we. Two, four, six, eight, we're offing ourselves before it's too late.' Word of the suicide swept the town, and three JV cheerleaders killed themselves the following weekend in the exact same spot. The girl who escaped was too afraid to tell the police what happened, and Tina's father was never implicated for any crime. In fact, he might still be loose in the woods tonight." She looked around at the group with an evil glare. "Who knows?"

"That didn't really happen," Tyson commented.

"Did too," Daisy said. "I've heard the story told many times. It's the truth."

"It's like something out of a *Daria* episode," I said. "Or that old movie *Heathers*. Total black humor. It's just a story."

"Whatever," Stephanie said. "True or not, it gives me the willies. My cousin's a cheerleader."

"Close enough," Dirk teased. He nudged me. "I'll protect you if someone comes in your tent tonight."

"Well, I've got one, guys," Ryan announced suddenly.

"Go ahead," Wes said.

"Okay, it's like this," Ryan began in a creepy tone of voice. "There are these four seniors on this end-of-school camping trip, right? Two guys: Jim and Trey, and two girls: Blake and Jude. They're having the time of their lives. Rafting on the river, eating marshmallows around a campfire like this one, talking into the wee hours of the night. A picture-perfect scene. Just like this one. They finally decide to go to sleep."

"Keep it clean, Baron," Wes warned, smiling.

"Of course—girls in one tent, guys in the other," Ryan said innocently, and we all laughed. "So the girls are sleeping soundly when all of a sudden Blake hears this rattle." Ryan fished a Tic Tac box out of his pocket and began to rattle the mints for special effect. "It's this loud, annoying rattle. She starts freaking out and nudges Jude, who's sound asleep. 'Listen,' Blake says. 'What could it be?' They don't want to scream for the guys, in fear of the rattling thing coming after them. So they sit still and wait. And the rattling gets louder"—he shook his Tic Tacs more furiously—"and louder, until they can barely hear themselves think. Then over the rattles they hear this earth-shattering scream." He let out an earsplitting yell, and we all jumped. "It's Trey. 'Don't move,' he says. 'Your tent is covered with snakes.'"

I shuddered, not wanting to hear anything more. I had a full-blown phobia of snakes—just the thought of them made me cringe. "I hate snakes more than anything in the world," I interrupted. "Don't go on."

Dirk squeezed my shoulder, but Ryan just smiled devilishly and continued, "So the girls start going ballistic since their tent is covered by rattlesnakes. They're crying and yelling and the whole nine."

"Enough," I said, closing my eyes. I felt an arm around my shoulders—Dirk's no doubt. At that moment I didn't care whose arm it was; I just wanted the story to end.

"Then they hear Jim screaming, 'Oh, my gosh, they're everywhere!' The girls are pleading with the guys to kill the snakes or do something, anything. 'Help!' they're screaming. *'Help!'* But all they hear is Jim yelling that they're going to get help, then the sound of the guys' hurried footsteps getting fainter and fainter as the rattles get louder and louder. They figure they're safe since there's no way into the tent. But then Blake remembers the tent tore earlier when she was assembling it, right in the corner. 'Oh, no!' she yells, grabbing something to obstruct the entry. And just as she's about to stuff the hole with her sweatshirt, a snake slithers in."

Completely terrified, I buried my head in my hands. I started to feel as though snakes were all around. What if one came in my tent tonight?

"Then another," Ryan went on. "Then another. By the time the guys come back for help, the tent is filled with snakes and both girls are dead." Ryan paused, and a scary silence fell over the group. I lifted my head slowly. "So guess what it said on their tombstone?"

"What?" Betty asked.

"Blake and Jude—Snake Food."

We all groaned at the corny one-liner. "That's horrible!" Daisy said, throwing a marshmallow Ryan's way.

"But I had you going, right?" he said.

131

I let out a heavy sigh, still shaken. "You had me going a little too well," I said, shuddering again. "The mere thought of snakes all over my tent will be enough to keep me up all night!"

Dirk hugged me tighter. "Don't worry, I'll be right next door," he said. Then he leaned and kissed my forehead.

I was so surprised by his gesture that it took me a moment to pull away. When I did, I said, "Thanks, you're a good friend." As I smiled at him I hoped he understood the meaning behind my words.

It was impossible for me to fall asleep that night, thanks to the visions of rattlesnakes dancing in my head. I'd been tossing and turning in my sleeping bag for hours, uncomfortable in the muggy tent, when I finally decided to get up and take a step outside into the fresh night air. As quietly as possible I slipped on my shorts and slithered out of the tent. But someone else was already outside—the moonlight illuminated the back of a guy's frame. *Dirk,* I figured.

I took a couple of small steps toward him. I definitely didn't want him to think that this was a romantic interlude or anything, but hopefully talking to him would get me over my miserable insomnia. *Just make it clear that you only want to be friends,* I told myself.

"Dirk," I whispered, tapping his shoulder.

But it was Ryan, not Dirk, who turned around.

"Sorry to disappoint," he said.

My heart felt like it accelerated to a thousand beats

a minute. "Ryan? What are you doing out here?"

He didn't answer for a moment, looking at the ground and running a hand through his hair. "Can't sleep," he grunted.

"Me neither," I whispered. I took a deep breath, trying to slow my racing pulse. This was it. This was my chance to tell Ryan everything.

I opened my mouth to speak, then closed it, feeling scared to death. Suddenly I remembered what my swimming teacher said to me when I was eight years old and frightened to jump off the high dive for the first time. "Don't think, just jump," he'd said. That was what I needed to do right now. I closed my eyes, gathering my strength, then opened them again. *Here goes,* I thought. "Ryan, there's something I need to tell you."

Ryan stared back at me—his expression was unreadable. He looked more serious than I'd ever seen him before. "I know what you're going to say, Brennan."

"You do?" I gasped, my hopes rising. "But how could you—"

"Stephanie likes me, right?" he interrupted in a gruff voice.

All my hopes came crashing down. "Wha-what?"

"Yeah," he said, taking a step back from me. "I figured it out a while ago. She's not my type or anything, but I'm flattered." He kicked around a small rock on the ground, shaking his head. "Although I can't believe such a good friend of yours would like me, seeing as I kicked your butt so majorly in the presidential election and all."

I stared back at him, not believing this was happening. I was about to bare my *soul* to this guy, and here he was insulting me? "You didn't exactly kick my butt," I said.

"Sure, I did." Ryan smirked. "But don't worry. I won't tell Dirkums."

"Tell *Dirkums* what?" I demanded, anger rising by the second. What was Ryan's deal?

"That I beat you so bad. I know how much you like him," Ryan said in a taunting voice.

That was it. I pulled Ryan away from the group of tents by the arm so that we wouldn't wake anyone up. "I do not like Dirk!" I insisted.

"Come on, Brennan." Ryan chuckled. "You do so. It couldn't be more obvious. You're always staring at him and asking for his help. 'Dirk, protect me from the big, bad, scary snakes,'" he imitated, breaking out into a falsetto.

Now I was furious. I had never sounded like that in my life! Was this what Ryan thought of me?

"'Dirkie, could you help me with this big, heavy bag,'" Ryan went on.

I shook my head angrily, not believing that I ever, even for a second, thought that I liked him. Obviously he hadn't changed a bit from the jerk I'd hated for years. And to think I was going to lay it all on the line for him!

I blinked back the tears of rage and disappointment. "I don't know what universe you're living in, Ryan," I snapped, "but you are seriously whacked. I am not

134

now, nor have I *ever* been, a damsel in distress!"

He snorted. "You're the queen of 'em, honey. A regular Scarlett O'Hara."

"Scarlett O'Hara was no damsel in distress, stupid, and neither am I," I said, fuming. "And don't flatter yourself by thinking Steph likes you. You are no Rhett Butler in anyone's book, you arrogant, egotistical jerk!"

I turned on my heel before Ryan had a chance to respond and stomped back to my tent. As I crawled inside I was tempted to wake Steph up. But the last thing I wanted was for Ryan to overhear our conversation—Steph would maybe mention the feelings I once had for him. *Once*. Those feelings were past tense now. Very past tense.

I buried my head under the sleeping bag and shut my eyes tight, trying desperately to erase Ryan's image from my mind. But it was useless—all the mean things he had said shot around my head like bullets. Who did he think he was, saying I always sought Dirk's approval? Not to mention rubbing it in about the election.

A single tear rolled down my cheek. Here I was thinking that there actually might be something between us, while all along he just thought I acted like a silly girl. How could he be so mean? My only consolation was that he showed his true colors *before* I confessed my feelings to him and made the mistake of my life.

But as the tears started streaming down my cheeks like rain, that didn't feel like much of a consolation at all.

Nine

"KYLIE, COME ON, time to get up," Steph said.

I had never felt more horrible than I did when Steph woke me up the following morning. Just the fact that Steph got out of bed before me illustrated what bad shape I was in. I squinted up at her, my head pounding and my eyes glued together from all the tears that I had shed the night before. In a flash last night's events came flooding back to me, and anger reached every cell of my body.

Ryan Baron caused me to cry two times in my life, I realized. *And I hate to cry. I never cry.* I buried my head back in my sleeping bag, remembering the way Ryan had smirked at me. "I hate him," I muttered.

"You hate who?" Steph asked.

I lifted my head up and looked at her.

"What's wrong with you?" she whispered. "You look like death."

"Thanks a lot," I whispered sarcastically, speaking in hushed tones in case Ryan was nearby. "You're never going to believe what happened."

Stephanie's eyes widened. "This sounds big."

As she dropped down next to me I told her about the Ryan encounter, sparing no details.

When I finished, Steph was in shock. "Oh, my gosh, I can't believe that," she gasped, her face draining of all color. "That's horrible."

"Tell me about it." I shook my head. "It's so unreal that he actually said all those things. That he was that mean." Then I had a horrible thought. "I don't really sound that way with Dirk, do I?"

"Of course not!" she insisted. "Ryan couldn't be more wrong." Her features clouded over with confusion. "I just don't get it. He was always asking about you and looking at you; that wasn't my imagination. And to think he sounded all cocky about me liking him—which I don't anymore anyway. The guy was wigging out."

"He was," I said, "but at least I don't have to worry about him anymore. Whatever I felt for him has been totally erased as of last night. I'm over it."

"Are you sure, Kylie?" Steph asked, searching my face. "Your feelings for him were pretty strong. How can they just go away, just like that?"

"Trust me—when a guy steps on you, it's easy to forget him. Especially if you never even had a relationship in the first place. Which we didn't."

Stephanie sighed. "This just blows. And I encouraged you to go for him! I feel so bad."

I shrugged. "It's not your fault, Steph. It's no-body's fault but Ryan's. He's the one who ruined what could have been the best thing he ever had. But now he'll never know."

"What are you going to do?" she asked.

"Thank my lucky stars I never told Ryan I liked him and avoid him like the plague for the rest of the trip."

"But you'll have to talk to him sometimes," Steph pointed out. "I mean, it's such a small group."

I stood up, thinking over her words. "Well, I guess you're right. I'll be civil to him if need be, but that's it. No good morning hellos, no more chitchat, nothing. I'm serious."

"That's right!" Steph exclaimed, standing up next to me. "He obviously doesn't deserve you anyway."

"Five minutes," Wes hollered from outside.

"That's our cue," I said, my stomach doing flip-flops. I dreaded facing Ryan, even if I was just going to ignore him.

"Let's get gorgeous," Steph said, giving me a quick hug.

I hugged her back, thankful for her friendship. At least there was one person on this trip who cared about my feelings.

As I exited the tent and stepped out into the early morning sunshine, I was energized by a newfound strength. I took a moment to absorb all the beauty of the campground—the red bluffs that surrounded us on all sides, the bright blue sky, the tranquility of it all. I was determined not to let Ryan Baron break me.

Taking a deep breath, I walked up to the group and smiled, saying hi to everyone. I was careful to avoid Ryan's gaze, which wasn't too hard because he was also looking everywhere but at me.

I dished out some granola, concentrating on the leaf-covered ground, the bird sounds. Anything to get my mind off *him*. Stephanie came beside me to get her breakfast. Then she cleared her throat and said, "Um, in case anyone's wondering, I don't like Ryan. I've heard some rumors to that effect, so I just wanted to clear that up."

I almost dropped my bowl of granola. I couldn't believe Steph had the nerve to say that! She just smiled, giving me a wink.

I turned around to look at how the group was reacting. They were tittering nervously and shifting their gaze from Stephanie to Ryan, who was blushing. Trying to save face, he said, "Oh, you don't, Steph? I thought every female on this trip had the hots for me." Then he flexed his muscles comically, and everyone laughed. Everyone except me, that is. I just stared down at my granola.

"My boyfriend wouldn't be too happy to hear that," Betty said, giggling.

Daisy laughed. "Hate to break it to you, Ryan, but you're too preppy for me. I only go for guys who have dreds."

"Maybe I better grow the hair out," he joked.

"What about you, Kylie?" Tyson asked. "You got the hots for Baron?"

"In his dreams," I said quickly, trying to cover

my embarrassment. "I wouldn't go out with him if he were the last guy on earth."

Ryan laughed as if it was all one big joke, but I did detect some hurt in his expression. *Good.* I hoped I'd hurt him as much as he'd hurt me last night.

Then, wanting to change the subject before things got out of hand, I said, "Wes, what's on tap for today?"

"Interesting segue," Wes said, winking. "But I'm glad you asked. We're going to load everything up here, hike back to the Suburban, then drive to Yellowstone. Once we arrive, you'll have a chance to see Old Faithful and do a few of the touristy things in the park. Then we'll hike out to our campsite for the night, which is a bit off the beaten trail."

As everyone cheered and gave their approval for the plan I took a big bite of granola. Seeing Ryan this morning had ruined my appetite, but he didn't have to know that.

Nope, around him I was going to act like the hungriest and happiest girl in the world.

Everyone was in great spirits as we hiked to our campsite at the end of the day, comparing notes about what we'd seen. When we'd arrived at Old Faithful that morning, we'd split into two groups—girls and guys—in order to walk around and explore. That was perfect for me since I could really take in all the beauty of Yellowstone without having to worry about Ryan being around.

"Could you guys believe the size of that thing?"

140

Daisy asked, ducking to miss a low branch on the flat, unpopulated trail.

"It's pretty amazing," Tyson agreed. "How about the number of people that were there? That was crazy."

"All tourist traps are like that," Betty said. "Yellowstone is kind of like Disneyland, nature style. What'd you think of the food court?"

"That was the highlight for me," Ryan said. "Junk-food-o-rama. Pretzels with cheese and pepperoni pizza."

"Yeah, and jumbo Coke," Dirk put in. "Did you guys get the chance to chow?"

I nodded. "Even though we've only been on the trip for five days, it felt like forever since I'd had junk food. I practically inhaled my turkey sub."

"I hope you guys didn't overdo it on that stuff," Wes said, looking back at us. "We've got a hard hike ahead in this backcountry, and tomorrow is going to be our toughest challenge yet."

"Don't worry—we'll make it," Ryan assured him. "But what's up for tomorrow?"

"That's for me to know and you to find out," Wes responded. "I have a little surprise for you all."

"A surprise, huh?" Betty said.

"And don't try to pry it out of me either," Wes advised, "because these lips are sealed."

The rest of the way to the campsite I hung back so that I'd be a considerable distance behind Ryan. As much as I hated to admit it, it still hurt to look at him.

Daisy hung back with me. "How are you doing, Kylie?" she asked.

"Oh, I'm fine," I lied.

"That's good," Daisy responded. The two of us hiked in silence for a little while, the only sound being the leaves crunching under our feet, until Daisy glanced at me and said, "I don't mean to pry, but I just have to tell you, I detect some real negative energy between you and Ryan."

I raised my eyebrows, surprised. "How could you tell?"

"You guys used to play around together so much—I thought that there might be something going on between you."

"Really?"

"Yeah, but now I sense that you're really hurt by something he's done."

I stared back at her, wondering if she'd eavesdropped on us last night. "How do you sense that?"

"It's your aura, Kylie. It's been damaged by someone, and I think that someone is Ryan."

Oh, great, I thought, squinting up at the sun. Not only had he wrecked my life, but he'd damaged my aura as well. Whatever the heck that was.

"Well, something did go down with Ryan and me, but I'd rather not discuss the details," I told her.

"Of course." Daisy shook her head. "I'm not after the dirt. I just want to help you cleanse yourself in some way—you know, heal your wounds."

"And how would you do that?" I asked, smiling. "Soap and water?"

She laughed. "All I'm saying is that I think you need to talk to him to make it right."

"There's no use. We have nothing to say to each other."

"But you need closure," she insisted. "That's important."

I felt like I was talking to someone from The Psychic Friends Network or something, but I decided to see where this aura stuff led me. "You really think I should talk to him?"

"Talk to who?" asked Steph, who we had suddenly caught up with.

"Ryan," I explained. "Daisy doesn't know the details, but she thinks I need closure."

"Closure, shmosure," Steph commented. "If Daisy knew the whole story, she wouldn't encourage you to talk to him. He's a total jerk!"

"I know," I said, sighing. But just because Ryan Baron was a jerk didn't mean that I should suffer. Maybe if I confronted him once and for all and gave him a piece of my mind, I'd feel better.

"But he's sabotaging his own happiness. And yours too," Daisy said to me.

"Let's just drop it," I said, getting a headache from this whole conversation. "I know I'll have to deal with him eventually. But until that opportunity presents itself, I'd just rather not waste one single brain cell on Ryan Baron, okay?"

Steph and Daisy both nodded, and the three of us continued the hike in silence. And with all the chaotic thoughts that were swirling around my brain, silence was exactly what I needed.

*   *   *

We didn't have any trouble finding wood for the campfire that night, as our campsite was right in the middle of a dense forest.

"This is wild!" Betty exclaimed.

"Isn't it beautiful?" Daisy sang, looking up at the sky and spinning around and around.

It *was* beautiful. We were surrounded by enormous, towering trees, the ground was covered with leaves and fallen bark, and since the tall trees provided shade, the air was refreshingly cool. Being in such a tranquil place had really helped to relax me. I'd managed to avoid Ryan for the last couple of hours and was enjoying soaking up all the incredible nature around me.

"This is sort of uncharted territory," Wes explained, building up the fire. "So it's pretty special."

"It makes me feel like we're the only people on the planet," said Tyson.

"Yeah," Dirk agreed. "I could stay here forever."

I stood close to the fire, watching it crackle and spark, thinking that I had to agree with Dirk. Being in such an isolated place really made all your everyday annoyances seem minuscule and irrelevant. Here you could truly concentrate on simply making the most of being alive.

As the campfire got roaring we opened up cans of tuna and boiled water for couscous. "I'm glad we're eating light," Stephanie said, "after all that Old Faithful food."

"Me too," I agreed. "I felt like I might lose my cookies earlier, hiking on such a full stomach."

Ryan glared at me from across the campfire.

"You'd know all about losing, wouldn't you, Kylie?"

I shot him a look. He wasn't going to start with me now, was he? "What are you talking about?" I demanded.

"You know, you lost the election last month, you lost your temper last night—what will you lose next?"

What was his problem? "My *mind* if I have to listen to you one more second!" I exclaimed.

"I'll do you a favor, then," he snapped. "I'm eating in my tent." Then he stomped away, carrying a can of tuna.

Everyone watched him walk away, then looked back at me, shocked. I met Stephanie's gaze and rolled my eyes.

"What was that all about?" Wes asked.

"Long story," I said, frustrated.

"Well, after we eat, let's talk for a second," Wes said.

I nodded, even though that was the last thing I wanted to do. But it wasn't like I could say no to Wes.

Dinner went by in a fog. As the sky got darker and darker everyone talked to me in these forced, polite tones, like they were talking to someone who might explode at any moment. Which I guess I might have. Ryan had officially pushed me over the edge.

After I pushed my tuna and couscous around the Star-Kist can for a while, I got up and approached Wes. "You ready to have that powwow?"

He nodded and told the group we'd be right back. He shone his flashlight as we walked to the farthest edge of the site, out of everyone's earshot. "What's going on with you and Ryan?" he asked as we sat down on a giant log. "You two seem to be having some real problems."

"That's an understatement," I said, kicking at the dirt with my foot.

"How did it all happen?"

I sighed. "You know Ryan and I go to the same school, right?"

Wes nodded.

"Well, we never really got along too well," I explained. "We've always been in all the same classes and we've always competed and fought with each other like crazy. And just before this trip, Ryan beat me out for student body president."

"Ouch."

"Yeah." I nodded. "Unfairly, too, I might add."

"But I have to tell you," Wes said, "you coulda fooled me. I thought you guys liked to hang out. You seemed to have a lot of fun that day we went fishing."

"Um, yeah." I was grateful that it was dark outside so that Wes couldn't see me blush. "We sort of started to get along. I guess being outside of school allowed me to see him in a new light and realize that there were things that were pretty cool about him."

"That's pretty common on these trips," Wes told me. "Actually, that's part of the reason I love them so much—it's cool to see all these different types of people bond and learn about each other." He smiled. "You know, I met my girlfriend when I was a camper on Adventure Trails."

"Really?" I asked, intrigued.

He nodded. "And I don't know if we would

have ever gotten together under other circumstances. We're pretty different."

"Wow," I said, trying to picture what Wes's girlfriend looked like. She was probably beautiful and superathletic. "What's her name?"

"Lori," Wes said. Then he shook his head. "We're talking about you, not me, remember?"

I shrugged. "I was hoping to get off easy."

"No, I'm going to get to the bottom of this. Now, the last thing you told me was that you two were getting along. So what happened?"

"What happened was that Ryan turned back into the jerk I hated at school . . . times twenty. I couldn't believe it; it was like Jekyll and Hyde. One minute we're playing around and laughing, and the next minute he's telling me that I act like a helpless female and try to get Dirk to do everything for me. He said some really mean things to me."

Wes raised his eyebrows. "What do you think prompted this outburst?"

"I have no idea," I responded. "Like I said, I thought we were really starting to get along. I guess I was wrong."

"This is obviously about something deeper," Wes said, scratching his forehead. "For him to have done a one-eighty like this, *something* must have happened."

"I don't know what it was," I said. "And honestly, I don't really care at this point. I'm just gonna steer clear of him for the rest of the trip."

"But there's still almost two weeks of Adventure Trails left," Wes said. "I'd hate for you both to have a miserable time because you're at each other's throats. I think you should talk to him, clear this up."

I shook my head. "I was thinking about that," I told him. "But after tonight I really think that talking won't do any good. But I promise there won't be any more scenes like tonight . . . at least if I can help it."

"All right," Wes said, not sounding convinced. "But think about what I said—there has to be a reason for all of this. And now that you know it is possible for you guys to get along, it could really be worth it to make that happen again. Not just for the rest of this trip but for the rest of high school too." He stood up. "There really might be something there for you two."

I stared up at him, trying to absorb his words. What exactly did he mean by "something" between us?

"Ready to go back?" Wes asked.

I nodded, standing up. *Well,* I thought, *whatever he does mean, it doesn't matter. Because there's no way I'm going to work things out with Ryan.* No way.

Ten

WES LET US sleep late the next morning, which was a much-appreciated luxury. Last night there had been an intense storm, which had fit my downcast mood perfectly. As I'd listened to the rain pound against our tent I'd fallen into a deep slumber, finally getting a good night's sleep.

So I was feeling well rested as I sat outside with the rest of the group, eating my bowl of granola. The late morning sun peeked through the leaves and branches of the tall trees, shedding a dappled light over our campground. I was ready to start a bright new day.

"Okay, time for your surprise," Wes declared as we all finished up our breakfast.

I'd forgotten all about the surprise. I looked at him with anticipation, wondering what it could be.

I didn't have to wait long to find out. "We're having map skills orientation today," he said. His announcement was met with a round of blank stares.

"What's that?" Stephanie asked, wrinkling her nose. "Sounds kind of boring."

Wes chuckled. "Don't pass judgment just yet. This is usually everyone's favorite. How it works is after we clean our mess and pack up our gear, I'll pair all of you off. Every pair will get a map, each map featuring a different path, all of which gets you to the same destination. The goal is to be able to successfully read the map and find your way there before sundown. And the first team to make it to the site wins a new, shiny compass." He paused. "Still sound boring?"

The group laughed. I was psyched—this activity sounded like the most challenging yet!

"I take it back," Stephanie said, smiling. "Do we get to choose our own partners?"

"Nope, I've already done that," he said. "Since there's an odd number of you, one lucky person is going to get me as a partner. But to keep it fair, I'll offer limited assistance. So let's pack up, then we'll get started."

Everyone jumped up and began to bustle around the campground, wanting to get going as soon as possible. As Stephanie and I disassembled our tent I wondered who my partner would be. I knew I was safe from being paired up with Ryan since Wes and I had talked about him last night.

Once the campground was clean and we were all packed up, Wes called us over. "Okay, guys, here we go," Wes said, maps in hand. "And no peeking at the maps till I say to. First team, Stephanie and Dirk."

They yelled in delight and grabbed their map from

Wes's hand. "We're gonna dominate!" Dirk declared, crouching down into a classic bodybuilder pose.

"Group two, Tyson and Daisy."

They smiled and cheered as they ran up to retrieve their maps. I smiled too—this meant I'd get Wes. Awesome.

"Group three, Kylie and Ryan."

What? The group fell silent, and my knees felt like they were going to give. How could Wes do this to me, especially after I spilled my guts to him last night? I glared at him, searching for answers, but all I got was a gentle smile as I angrily snatched the map from his outstretched hand.

This is going to be pure torture, I thought, glancing over at Ryan. He didn't look any happier than I did. He was scowling, intently staring down at his Timberland-covered feet. *It's all his fault we're in this predicament anyway,* I thought. If Ryan hadn't caused that outburst last night, Wes never would've hatched this twisted plot to pair us up so we'd make up or talk or something. Which wasn't going to happen. Not in this lifetime.

"So, Betty, you're stuck with me," Wes said, handing her the last map. "Now, here are some things to remember: One, stay calm; two, trust your compass and instincts; three, don't kill your partner; and four, have your first aid kit on the ready at all times." He paused. "Any questions?"

"Yeah, I've got one," Tyson said. "Are y'all ready to have your butts kicked by Daisy and me?"

Tyson's challenge elicited loud protests from

everyone but Ryan and me—we just stood there silently fuming. After a moment Wes told everyone to pipe down, then issued his closing remarks: "Be careful and safe, and I'll see you by sundown. On your mark, get set, go!"

Everyone opened their maps in a flurry, then hurriedly dispersed in different directions. Ryan and I exchanged an angry glare, then slowly and quietly looked over our map.

"I guess we need to go that way," Ryan mumbled after a moment, pointing to a trail to the left.

"I guess," I agreed, starting to walk in that direction. As we headed to the trail in silence I once again cursed my bad luck. Why out of six potential partners did I have to end up with the biggest jerk on the planet? *Because of Wes,* I reminded myself, my hands clenching into fists. If I survived this day with Ryan, I would never let Wes hear the end of it.

Eventually Ryan broke the heavy silence. "I bet you're pretty mad you didn't get lover boy Dirk as your partner, huh?" he asked.

"Mind your own business," I said, figuring it was pointless to argue. If Ryan wanted to think I was in love with Dirk, that was his problem.

Those were the last words exchanged between us for a long time. For the next couple of hours or so Ryan and I shared nothing but directional information. Our silence seemed overwhelming at times—the only noise we made was the sound of our footsteps crunching on the leaves and dead branches. I concentrated on taking in all the beauty of the tree-lined trail that we were on, trying to get something positive out of this whole experience. Thank God the map had been pretty easy to follow, and we'd had no major disagreements.

Curious as to where we were, I grabbed the map out of Ryan's hands and inspected it, mentally noting that we'd need to make a turn in a short while.

"You look like that woman from *I Dream of Jeannie*," Ryan commented, referring to the high ponytail my hair was in. I was surprised to hear him utter a real sentence, but of course it was a stupid insult. Now I knew why I hadn't been talking to him—he was an idiot.

"At least I don't look like a pirate minus the patch," I said, pointing to the bandanna on his head.

He rolled his eyes. "You gonna grant me three wishes, Jeannie?"

"Sure, as long as wishes one, two, and three involve you disappearing."

Without responding, Ryan bent down to retrieve a walking stick. It actually wasn't such a bad idea since the brush was getting kind of thick. "You should find one too," he said gruffly.

"I guess you're right," I admitted quietly, stopping to look for a stick of my own. Unfortunately I was having no luck.

"Need some help?"

"Not from you," I snapped.

"Why do you have to be so defensive all the time?" Ryan grabbed a stick from the ground and practically flung it at me.

"Why do you have to be so obnoxious?" I asked, leaning on the stick as I trudged forward. "First you call me a damsel in distress, then you say I'm defensive when I won't accept your help. How can I win?"

"You're crazy," he muttered.

I quickened my pace so that I was two or three steps ahead of Ryan. I'd decided that moving at different speeds was our best bet for making it through the day without punching each other out. Because if I had to stand next to him for one more single second, I wasn't sure *what* I'd do.

Soon we approached the landmark that signaled we needed to turn right. There was just one little problem: Ryan insisted we needed to turn left.

"Look at the map," I said, pointing it out to him. "It's obvious. See? We need to turn right here."

"You're looking at it totally wrong." Ryan turned the map upside down. "We started here, see? And then we went that way, then that way. We already made that right turn. Now we need to veer left."

I shook my head. "You've got it backward. And I'm not just saying that because I'm talking to . . . well, you. I'm being serious."

Ryan sighed loudly. "Let's flip for it. Heads I win, tails you lose."

I shrugged—anything was better than wasting our time arguing. "You got a coin?"

He pulled a penny out of his pocket. "I'll flip, you call," he said, tossing the coin into the air.

"Heads!" I called. I was relieved to see that when the penny hit the ground, Lincoln's profile was faceup.

"Okay, okay, you win," Ryan said. "But when we turn around because we're lost, don't say I didn't tell you so."

"Whatever," I said, turning right and leading us down what I was more than certain was the correct path.

But after a little while my confidence began to wane—the terrain was getting very rocky, and the brush was getting thicker and thicker. "This is definitely not the right way," Ryan said from behind me. "Wes would never send us through something like this."

"Quit acting like such a know-it-all," I snapped, even though I was starting to fear he might be right.

"I will—when you stop acting like a stuck-up princess," he growled.

Ryan and I continued along the bumpy path in silence, which was getting bumpier and bumpier by the minute. We even had to climb over some huge rocks. And my walking stick wasn't much help.

As much as I hated to admit it, I'd been wrong. I let out a deep breath and stopped walking. "I guess we better turn back," I said, voice small. Those were the six hardest words I'd ever uttered, I swear.

Ryan rolled his eyes and put his hands on his hips. "Oh, that's beautiful, Brennan, just beautiful. We wouldn't be in this mess if you listened to me in the first place."

"Spare me the lecture," I said. I turned around and stomped forward past him. "I made a mistake. I'm sorry I'm not as perfect as you, Mr. President."

"That's obvious." He snorted.

I chose to ignore his comment and kept walking. I let out a heavy sigh as I reached the group of big rocks that we'd traversed before—I was not looking forward to climbing them again.

"Be careful," Ryan called.

What did he think I was—an idiot? Well, I'd show him. I climbed up the rocks with a burst of energy, jumping off like I was a pro. But I didn't feel like anything except a klutz when I lost my balance on landing, twisting my ankle and falling facedown. A searing pain shot up my ankle.

"Aaaaah!" I screamed.

Ryan jumped the rocks and rushed over to me. "Are you okay? What hurts?"

"My ankle!" I cried, blinking back tears. "My ankle!"

"Let me take a look at it," he said. He sat down next to me, helping me to remove my backpack. Then he felt my ankle gingerly. "Does this hurt?"

"No."

"How about this?"

"Aaaah!" I screamed.

"There's my answer," Ryan said, lessening the pressure. "Looks like you twisted it pretty bad, Brennan."

I shook my head. "I couldn't have," I insisted, even though my ankle was still throbbing. "I'm sure I can still go on."

Ryan looked skeptical. "I don't think so. But let's try to put some pressure on it to be sure." He hopped up, then slowly helped me up. "Okay, place your foot on the ground and put your weight on it."

I bit my lip and followed his instructions. "Okay," I said. "It's fine. It's—*aaaaaah!*"

"Definitely sprained," Ryan confirmed, "maybe even broken. Here—lean on me."

"Perfect," I complained, shifting all my weight onto him, "just perfect."

"We need to find somewhere for you to rest." Ryan glanced around our surroundings, assessing the situation. "All right, see that clearing over there?" He pointed to a narrow opening in the brush to the left of the trail, which appeared to lead into a large clearing.

"Uh-huh."

"We'll head over there. Ready?"

I nodded forlornly.

"Let's go. Don't put any weight on your foot— keep leaning on me," Ryan instructed.

"Okay," I mumbled. Cursing myself, I was silent as Ryan helped me hobble through the brush and into the wide open clearing. He then lowered my body onto a patch of grass. I winced as my entire leg began to throb. I had never felt as helpless as I did at that moment.

Ryan knelt down next to me. "Oh, God," I said. I turned my head away from Ryan so that he couldn't see me wiping my tears. "I can't believe this, I really can't."

"Don't freak, Brennan," he said. "We gotta stay calm."

How could I stay calm when I had an injured

ankle and had to depend completely on Ryan? In a minute he'd be saying that this never would have happened if I'd listened to him, that I was beyond clumsy. I glanced at him. "Go ahead—tell me I'm a dumb klutz and this is all my fault."

He looked startled. "I would never do that." Then he began to fumble around in his backpack for the first aid kit. "Okay, here's some gauze," he said. "Let's wrap that ankle up nice and tight."

As he went to work wrapping my rapidly swelling ankle I began to panic. No one knew where we were. We were completely isolated. I couldn't walk. "What are we going to do?"

Ryan shook his head. "I don't know."

Great. Neither of us had an idea. "Well, that's a first," I muttered.

"Why, you ungrateful—" Ryan stopped himself midsentence and took a deep breath. "Listen, Brennan, I know we don't exactly, um, like each other, but we're in an emergency situation here. We have to work together now if we want to get through this."

"You're right," I responded quietly. "God, this is such a nightmare," I said, rubbing my ankle tenderly.

"I wish it was." Ryan gave me his signature half smile—something I hadn't seen in a while. "At least then we could wake up and it would all be over."

"Right," I said, chuckling a little despite myself. "Ouch—my ankle hurts more when I laugh."

"I'll chill on the jokes, then. And let's get you some aspirin." He handed me two white tablets.

"That should take some of the edge off."

I washed them down with a sip from my canteen, the water warm and metallic tasting. The pain shooting through my ankle felt like it was getting worse. I let out a shaky sigh. "I'm kinda scared."

"I have to admit I'm not feeling too great about this either," Ryan said, looking around our desolate surroundings. "I'm going to have to go get some help."

The thought of being out there alone was beyond terrifying. "Please don't leave me out here," I pleaded, not caring anymore if Ryan thought I acted like a damsel in distress. "If anything happens, I won't be able to move. And what if you can't find your way back to me?"

Ryan nodded. "Okay, I'll stay," he told me. "Wes will find us out here. He must know all these trails like the back of his hand." He wiped his brow with his bandanna. "Don't worry, it'll be fine."

"Hopefully," I said.

"How's the ankle feeling?" he asked. "Any better?"

"It hurts, but I guess I'll live. That is, if we're not eaten by wild animals before we're rescued," I moaned, only half kidding.

Ryan rolled his eyes. "Don't be such a baby," he said. "Nothing is going to happen to us."

I stared back at him angrily. "I can't believe you would call me a baby when I'm sitting here with a possibly broken, definitely sprained ankle in ninety-degree weather with no medical attention, no hope of rescue, nothing! That is totally uncalled for."

Ryan bit his lip. "You know what, I'm sorry,"

he said. "I shouldn't have said that. It was totally rude."

"Then why'd you say it?" I asked.

"Because we're stuck out here and there's nothing we can do about it, which is pretty much killing me," he explained. "In case you haven't noticed, I'm a bit of a control freak."

"I have noticed." I laughed. "But I can relate. *You* might have noticed that I'm the same way."

Ryan smiled. "I guess you are."

"My brother calls me In Charge Marge."

"Yeah?" Ryan lifted an eyebrow. "Thank God that's not *really* your name. Or else I might have to change mine to I Can Handle It, Man, Stan."

I laughed at his corny joke, then cringed in pain. "I told you not to make me laugh, Baron."

"Oops, I slipped. Won't happen again." He jumped up. "I'm going to get some wood while it's light out. That way we can start a fire if we're still out here when night falls. Will you be all right?"

I leaned back on a tree stump, tilting my head up to the sky—which was still bright blue. I prayed someone would find us before the sky darkened. Being stuck in an isolated forest with Ryan was not exactly how I wanted to spend an evening, even if he was on his best behavior. "Sure," I told him, "go ahead."

A few hours later we were sitting across from each other playing rock-paper-scissors when disaster struck—I had to go to the bathroom.

"Um, Ryan," I said, beyond embarrassed, "we've got, uh, a little problem."

"What's that?"

"Nature's calling, and I can't pick up," I said, hoping he didn't ask me to explain any further.

Ryan's eyes darted to the ground uncomfortably. But then he looked right back at me. "Well, how should we do this?"

"Why don't you walk me over to those bushes, then walk back and close your eyes and cover your ears," I suggested. "Wait about five minutes, then come retrieve me."

Ryan didn't make a joke about the situation or anything. He just nodded and helped me up, telling me not to put any pressure on my foot if I could help it.

"Oh, my gosh, it hurts," I complained, even though I was leaning most of my weight on him.

"I know it does, but we're not going very far—just to those bushes over there. You can do it."

As I hopped over to our destination the absurdity of the situation suddenly hit me. Ryan Baron—the guy who had been my enemy for years, then had turned into someone I sort of liked, then had been extremely mean to me, making me hate him once again—was now supporting my weight as I, mortified, hobbled over to a bush so that I could pee in the woods. I couldn't possibly be more dependent on the guy. I had to laugh out loud at how ridiculous it all was.

Ryan raised one eyebrow. "What's so funny?"

I shook my head. "I couldn't possibly explain."

"That's not fair."

"Life's not fair," I responded as we neared the bushes.

He eased me to the ground on the other side of the shrubbery. "There you go," he said. Then he started to walk away.

"Hey, Ryan," I called to him.

He turned around. "Yeah?"

"Thanks for being cool about all this."

He didn't respond for a moment. Then that half smile crept onto his face. "No problem," he said, "no problem at all."

An hour later Ryan and I were sitting in front of three campfires in triangular formation that Ryan had constructed earlier, which was what Wes had told us to do if we ever got lost. That way when helicopters spotted the formation from the air, they knew you needed help. And without Wes we needed all the help we could get. We didn't have any food either, unless you counted the peanut butter PowerBar that Ryan and I had split two hours ago.

"I'm so hungry," I complained, staring up at the pitch-black sky and the millions of stars that sparkled above.

"Let's not talk about it," Ryan said. "We need to distract ourselves."

"How? We've already played password and name that tune."

"How about we just talk?" Ryan suggested.

"Talk?" I repeated. "About what?"

"I don't know. Anything."

"All right," I said apprehensively. Ryan had been pretty cool through this all, but I still didn't want to share any secrets with him or anything.

Ryan hugged his knees against his chest. "So, who's your favorite teacher?"

"Of all time or last year?"

"Both."

Easy enough. "All time—Mrs. Lincoln, sixth-grade PE. Last year—Mr. Clark, English. You?"

"Um . . . all time—Ms. Samra, photography. Last year—Mr. Devareux, honors history."

"Devareux? Really?"

Ryan nodded. "He can be really tough, but I thought his class was awesome. I really learned a lot."

"I guess I did too, now that I think about it. He was just so stern all the time."

"Nah." Ryan smiled. "That's all an act. He's a real teddy bear inside."

"Devareux? He coulda fooled me."

"He fools most people," Ryan agreed, laughing. He stared at me for a moment, then said, "You know, it's funny. We've had all these classes together for years, and we hardly know anything about each other."

"Not true." I shook my head. "I know that you have a bad French accent, and I know that you couldn't do a chemistry experiment by yourself if your life depended on it."

Ryan lifted his eyebrows. "Watch it there, Brennan—right now your life depends on me." We both laughed. "Besides, you know that's not what I meant."

I shrugged. "What do you want to know?"

"Let's see . . . favorite color?"

"Deep purple."

"Light blue for me," he said. "Your turn to ask."

"Um . . . favorite movie?"

"*Scream II*," he answered instantly.

"That was good," I agreed. "But not as good as *I Know What You Did Last Summer*."

"Are you an *X-Files* fan?"

"Sci-fi's not my thing," I told him, yawning.

"But Scully's hot," he said. His blue eyes lit up with amusement.

"Well, Mulder's not so bad either."

"Touché." Ryan smiled, and we were both quiet for a moment.

The only sound was the gentle rustling of the leaves in the light wind. I picked up a small twig and twirled it around my fingers.

"What about personal stuff?" Ryan asked, breaking the silence.

Startled, I stared back at him. "Like what?"

"I don't know." He shrugged. "Like, uh, have you ever had a serious boyfriend?"

"Not exactly," I said slowly. "I mean, I've dated some guys, but none of them were too serious." I looked down, using the twig to trace lines in the soft dirt. "How about you? Didn't you go out with that foreign exchange student last year?"

"Brittany?" he asked. I nodded. "Yeah," he said. "It never got that serious. Although I was really bummed when she went back to Holland."

"That must've been hard," I said, yawning again. I'd never really known Brittany, but an image of Ryan walking down the halls with her—a beautiful brown-haired girl—now popped into my mind.

"Kind of," he admitted, running a hand through his hair. "But for me school has always come first anyway. You know how it is."

"Yep, gotta be the best." I nodded sleepily. "It's difficult sometimes."

"Tell me about it." He smiled. "You know, there were times I wanted to throw in the towel on something, but I kept going just so you wouldn't beat me out."

"You too?" I laughed.

"Yeah," Ryan said, laughing along. "We're probably responsible for each other's success. Ironic, huh?"

I nodded, laughing even more. Then my eyes fell on Ryan's, and we stared at each other for a long moment, our laughter dying down. Suddenly I felt the same charged electricity that I'd experienced that day we'd gone fishing. But then just as quickly I remembered the mean things he'd said to me, the way he'd turned on me out of nowhere, and I snapped back to reality.

I averted my gaze and focused intently on the flickers of the campfire. "When are they gonna find us?" I muttered, hugging myself.

"Hopefully soon," he said softly. "But, uh, I'll keep these three fires burning until they do."

I closed my eyes, trying to erase the awkwardness I

felt between us. "I really appreciate everything you've done."

"No sweat."

"Mmm." My lids were getting heavier and heavier.

"You tired?"

"Not really," I mumbled. "I'm just resting my eyes for a few."

Hours later I woke up with a start to a strange sound, completely confused. Where was I? What was I doing here? And whose arms were around me? I glanced behind me and saw the arms were Ryan's. It all came rushing back—us getting lost, the nasty fall, the twisted ankle, the fact that we were all alone and no one had found us yet.

I carefully lifted Ryan's arms from my body, wondering how they got there. Had I used him as a human pillow last night?

There was that strange sound again. I rubbed my eyes against the breaking sunlight, looking around for the source of the noise. Whatever it was, it was annoying. It sounded like a maraca, or . . . someone shaking a Tic Tac box. Then all of a sudden I spotted a rattlesnake, slithering out from under my backpack, just ten feet away.

"Snake!" I screeched. "We're going to die!"

Ryan bolted up immediately. "What? Where?"

I pointed to the rattler. "Oh, no!" he said, leaping up and grabbing a stick.

"Snake! Snake!" I cried out, hysterical.

Ryan put his hand over my mouth. "Be quiet,"

he whispered in a shaky voice, "and don't panic." He approached the rattlesnake slowly, whispering, "It's going to be okay. It's going to be okay."

I couldn't tell if he was trying to comfort me or himself, but I was still a mess. I was shaking violently, certain the snake was going to attack me at any minute.

Ryan took another step toward the snake.

What would I do if the rattler bit Ryan? I held my breath as he inched closer, holding the stick out in front of him.

Ryan poked the snake with the stick very slowly. The rattler hissed in protest.

My whole body tensed up. "Oh, my God," I whispered.

Ryan slowly picked up the snake with the stick.

As the snake dangled from the flimsy piece of wood I covered my eyes with my hands. I heard a swoosh. When I looked up, the snake was flying in the air into the woods.

Ryan glanced back at me and dropped the stick to the ground. His face was pale, and his eyes were wide and bug-eyed.

He jogged over and collapsed next to me, shaking. I was still trembling too.

A huge wave of relief rushed over me. "You saved our lives!" I exclaimed, hugging him tightly.

"Thank God," he said, hugging me back.

Then I had a horrible thought. I pulled back from him slightly, still holding on to his shoulders. "Do you think it's going to come back?" I whispered.

Ryan shook his head, collecting his breath.

"Snakes are creatures of the night who seek warm places to sleep," he explained, "which is probably why Mr. Rattler parked under your backpack. I don't think he'll be back after that wake-up call."

I exhaled heavily. "Good."

Ryan pulled me back in a tight embrace, whispering, "I'm so glad we're okay."

He held the hug a beat too long, and I began to relax in his arms. I liked how it felt to be there. It felt safe . . . and comfortable.

All those feelings of attraction came flooding back, and I couldn't hold them in anymore. I didn't *want* to hold them in. And after what we'd been through, it seemed stupid to try to deny it. "Ryan, I have something to tell you," I whispered.

This time he was the one to pull away. Concern filled his light blue eyes. "What?"

"I don't know how to say this," I said, my voice trembling. I knew I had to go through with it. I had to clear the air and get this out there. "I, uh, sort of liked you."

His eyes widened, and his jaw dropped in surprise. But when he spoke, his voice was soft. "What are you saying?"

My cheeks burning, I looked down to the ground. "I mean, that night outside the tent, the night we fought . . . I was going to tell you—"

Ryan put his hand on my chin, gently tilting my head up and forcing me to look at him. "You were going to tell me you liked me?"

My heart hammering, I nodded.

"As in more than a friend?" he asked.

I nodded again, too terrified to speak.

"Wow." A smile began to form on his face. But that smile vanished quickly. "And then I was such a jerk . . ."

"Yes," I whispered, looking down. "You were."

"Brennan." Ryan put a hand on each of my shoulders, massaging them. "I only acted that way because I was totally jealous."

"Jealous?" I repeated, unable to stop the hope from creeping into my voice.

"Yes." Ryan nodded rapidly, his eyes pleading with mine. "I'm sorry I was such a jerk. But it's just that I had really started to, um, dig you"—Ryan's eyes darted away from mine for a moment and I smiled—"and I thought you liked Dirk. It was driving me crazy; I didn't know what to do."

"So you thought being completely obnoxious was a good solution," I accused him. But I was still smiling.

Ryan shook his head. "I was just so angry that you would like Dirk. I was stupid."

I nodded, smiling and holding his gaze with mine. "So stupid."

His blue eyes crinkled as he grinned. "So stupid," he repeated.

"Extremely stupid."

He nodded. "Extremely stupid."

"Extremely, ridiculously stupid."

"That's it, Brennan," Ryan teased, reaching for me and pulling me close to him—pulling me into a kiss.

The kiss was soft, sweet . . . and right. I didn't want

it to end. I wanted to remember everything about this moment—the morning sun peeking through the trees, the fresh, crisp smells of the forest, the soft feel of Ryan's hand against my cheek, I even wanted to remember my aching ankle—for the rest of my life.

Ryan slowly pulled away.

"So I guess you like me too?" I asked playfully, my heart skipping a beat.

"Yeah." He broke into a smile and nodded. "Big time."

Our lips met in another honey sweet kiss. Suddenly I didn't care if we were ever rescued.

I drew away, tracing Ryan's cheek with my finger. "This is so weird," I whispered.

Ryan looked at me questioningly.

"I mean weird in a good way," I assured him. "Who would of thought that you and I, former archenemies, would end up falling in love?"

"It is funny," Ryan whispered, wrapping a strand of my hair around his finger. "Although I have to say, I think that I liked you even when we were enemies."

"You *did?* But we fought all the time."

Ryan's eyes twinkled. "The real reason we argued so much is probably because we're so similar—we have the same goals, the same values."

"I guess that's true," I said softly, suddenly seeing things in a new light.

"And I've always had so much respect for you—you're a real fighter." He squeezed my shoulder, staring into my eyes. "You've always pushed me to do my best."

"You too," I told him. But something was still bothering me. "But the election—"

"I have to apologize for that." Ryan dropped his hands from my arms and shifted his eyes to the ground.

"No, you don't. I mean you won—"

"But not fairly." He lifted his eyes back up to mine. "I know that I cut corners. Not that it makes it right, but my father—he's a congressman—put a lot of pressure on me to win." Ryan sighed. "He puts a lot of pressure on me for everything, actually. But he told me the only way he'd send me on this trip was if I won the election."

"Wow," I whispered. I couldn't imagine my parents ever acting that way. "I had no idea."

"The whole time I felt really bad about my cheap tactics. And after the election I wanted to explain it to you to clear things up," Ryan continued. "Then I saw what you wrote in my yearbook, and I realized you didn't want to have anything to do with me."

"Oh, God," I said, cringing as I remembered my nasty letter. "I *was* horrible."

Ryan gave me a small smile. "You were. But you had every right to be." He took my hand in his. "And you know what? When we get home, I'm going to tell Principal Overman that I want you to be my co-president."

I squeezed his hand, touched by the gesture. "Ryan, that's very sweet. But I didn't win—you did."

"I didn't deserve to," he insisted. He paused for a moment. "Besides, you and I need to start working as a team rather than competing."

A rush of warmth came over me at his words. "That sounds good to me."

"Yeah?"

"Yeah." I smiled. "It's more than good. It's perfect."

Ryan's mouth drew up into a half smile—the same smile that used to drive me crazy in school. Actually, it still did drive me crazy . . . just in a different sort of way. Goose bumps traveled up my arm as I gazed back at him.

At that moment Wes's voice could be heard in the distance. "Ryan? Kylie?" he called.

Ryan and I exchanged looks of excitement. "We're saved!" I exclaimed.

Ryan jumped up. "Over here!" he called. "We're over here!"

"I hear you!" Wes bellowed.

"We're coming!" Steph's voice called out.

Ryan dropped down next to me, pulling me into a hug. "It's all over," he said. "They've found us!"

I let myself melt into his embrace. "There's one part about this that I don't want to be over," I whispered.

Ryan smiled. "Me either." We kissed again. A sweet, soft, lingering kiss.

"Kylie? Ryan?"

I broke away from Ryan to see Wes standing five feet away, watching us, hands on his hips.

Embarrassed, Ryan and I started to laugh. "Wes," Ryan said between chuckles, "we can explain."

"No need." Wes shook his head, smiling. "I figured this would happen."

"You *did?*" I asked.

"Uh-huh." Wes walked closer to us. "I figured that *this*"—his eyes darted from Ryan to me—"was the source of all your tension."

"Oh," I mumbled, a bit humiliated. "Guess you were right."

Steph and Dirk came running from the trail. "Are you guys okay?" Dirk asked as they neared us.

"Kylie!" Steph exclaimed, panting. "We were so worried!"

"So was I," Wes said. "But apparently there was no need to worry about these two . . . no need at all."

My cheeks began to flame up in response to Wes's teasing tone. Steph and Dirk looked from Ryan to me, confused.

It didn't take long for Steph to read my expression. "Oh, my God!" she exclaimed, running over and giving me a hug. "This is too perfect!"

Dirk still looked confused. "What am I missing?" he asked. "What's going on?"

Steph jumped up. "Kylie and Ryan like each other!" she squealed. "They're, like, together." A worried expression then crossed her features. "That's okay to say, right?" she asked me anxiously.

I laughed. "Yeah—it's all out in the open now."

"It's about time," Wes joked.

"Wow," Dirk mumbled, seemingly at a loss for words.

As I took in his dumbstruck reaction a funny thought popped into my head. "I wonder what Jenni will say when she finds out."

Steph smiled. "She's gonna flip!"

Then Wes noticed my ankle. "Kylie, what happened? Why is your foot all wrapped up?"

"Oh, I kind of sprained it."

"I think it might be broken," Ryan said, massaging my shoulders.

"All this talk about you and Ryan, and you're sitting here in pain." Wes crouched down beside me, concerned. "We've got to get you to a doctor."

"Does it hurt?" Dirk asked.

I nodded. "It's pretty sore."

"I'm so sorry," Steph told me. "That's horrible."

"She'll be fine," Wes said, standing up. He crossed his arms over his chest, thinking for a moment. "Okay. Here's what we'll do: Steph and Dirk, you go back and tell the others what's going on—I'll point out which way to go. Ryan, you come with me and Kylie to the Suburban. We'll take her to the hospital, then I'll come back to collect everyone else. Sound good?"

We all nodded.

"All right, then. Ryan, you think you can carry Kylie piggyback style to the car? We can switch off if you get tired."

"No problem," Ryan said.

"Good." Wes looked down at me. "You ready to stand up?"

I nodded. As Wes and Ryan helped me rise to my feet Dirk spoke up. "Hey—I have a question."

Leaning on Ryan, I glanced over at him.

"How did you guys get lost in the first place?"

Ryan and I locked eyes and grinned. "We couldn't agree on which path to take," I said after a moment.

Wes laughed. "Why am I not surprised?"

"But for the record," Ryan said, his eyebrows lifting teasingly, "I was right."

I shoved him playfully. "You just had to say that, didn't you?"

"Yes." Ryan nodded, laughing. "I did." Then he took my hand in his, his eyes becoming serious. "But you know what? I've never been so glad to get lost in my life."

"Me either, Ryan." I smiled back at him, feeling the happiness radiate throughout me. "Me either."

Do you ever wonder about falling in love? About members of the opposite sex? Do you need a little friendly advice but have no one to turn to? Well, that's where we come in . . . Jenny and Jake. Send us those questions you're dying to ask, and we'll give you the straight scoop on life and love in the nineties.

DEAR JAKE

Q: *I've known for a long time that I'm in love with my best friend, Cameron. I haven't told him how I feel because he says he doesn't believe in relationships. How can I get him to change his mind and see that we're perfect for each other?*

MB, Las Vegas, NV

A: Unfortunately guy-speak isn't always so easy to interpret. When Cameron says, "Oh, man, being single is the life," he could mean one of many things. Maybe he's been hurt before, and he thinks it's safer to avoid the danger zone. Maybe he's just shy, and he'd rather pretend he's not interested than wonder if anyone wants a relationship with him. Or—I know you don't want to hear this, but we must consider every possibility—it could be that Cameron is being totally honest, and he just doesn't feel ready to commit yet.

So how do you know what the truth is? As Cameron's best friend, you must know a lot about his past. Has he had any traumatic experiences with girls that left him broken and bleeding? Does he get timid around girls he doesn't know very well? If you can answer yes to either of these questions, then you need to try a little honesty with your friend. Ask him straight out why he avoids relationships. If he seems more flexible than he's been claiming to be, you have a chance. Just be sure to move slowly since the transition from a friend to a girlfriend can be complicated.

Q: *There are these two guys, Mike and Paul, that I like. I'm only fourteen, and I don't see why I should have to commit to anyone yet. I want to date them both, but the problem is that they're friends. Do you think there's any way I can do this?*

HP, Fort Wayne, IN

A: Let's see . . . convince two buddies to take turns going out with the same girl, meaning that they would have to calmly listen to each other describe the way you kiss while wondering which one of them you liked better? Hmmm, am I the only one who sees how completely *impossible* your idea is? I don't mean to be offensive, because I know that your intent is innocent enough and you are trying to go about things in the best possible way. However, there is no way to navigate this jungle without the three of you ending up scraped, bitten, and scarred. As tough as it may seem, you're going to have to choose whether you're more interested in Mike or Paul before letting them know anything. Maybe you'd rather keep them both as friends and date other people—you're right to say that there is no need for you to settle down with one guy when you're not ready for that. Whatever you decide, remember that getting in between friends is a surefire way to make all three of you lose.

Q: *I know that guys hate it when their girlfriends are too pushy, so I've always tried to give my boyfriend, Justin, plenty of space. But lately it just seems like he's always with his friends. I'm thinking of telling him that if he doesn't start spending more time with me, he won't be spending any because I'll break up with him. Is this a big mistake?*

CS, Shiro, TX

A: Obviously you're growing increasingly frustrated with Justin's lack of attention, and if this is the case, you have to let him know. However, you're right that guys are sensitive to anything that feels like control or nagging; ultimatums are generally a bad idea. Why don't you try explaining your feelings to Justin the way you did to me? Tell him that you do respect his need to have time alone or with other people but that doesn't mean he should take you for granted. Plus there's nothing wrong with making it clear that as willing as you are to compromise, you're not going to be happy with the relationship if he doesn't make an effort to change his behavior. You have a right to ask this much of him.

DEAR JENNY

Q: *A friend of mine knew this guy that she thought I'd get along with, so she gave him my phone number. He called me, and we totally hit it off—we've been talking for hours every night. He wants to meet me in person, but I'm worried that things won't be the same face-to-face. Is it possible to fall in love with someone you've never met?*

CW, Tucson, AZ

A: Have you ever seen *Sleepless in Seattle?* One of my biggest fantasies has always been to "meet" the love of my life before ever seeing his face and just know that he's the right guy. I understand why you're concerned about seeing this guy in person when you're used to him just being a voice over the telephone. Certainly things will be a little awkward at first while you both adjust to the new dimension. However, are you willing to risk never knowing if this guy is "the one" in order to avoid a bit of nervousness? You already know that you have plenty in common and can keep each other entertained for long periods of time. The worst-case scenario is that the physical attraction isn't quite right, and then you'll still gain a good friend. My one suggestion is that you meet in a public place (these days you can't be too careful) and in a casual, low-pressure atmosphere, like a fun restaurant.

Q: *I like this guy, Chris, and I know he likes me too. The problem is that I get really shy whenever we're alone together, and I can't seem to find anything to say to him. When we're in a big crowd, I have no trouble talking, but one-on-one makes me so nervous. What can I do to get over this so that I can go on a date with him?*

RT, Chicago, IL

A: You poor thing! I know just what you mean—I used to get totally tongue-tied around guys I liked, and I didn't understand why I would change from being my usual articulate, charming self into a stuttering glob of Jell-O. Then I learned the key to overcoming my shyness: Fake it. That's right, before you can become comfortable spending time alone with your guy, you have to pretend to both him and yourself that you've never felt calmer. As silly as it sounds, it can actually help to brainstorm conversation topics before your big date so that you already have ideas of what to say when you're together. Another helpful option is to make a movie the first event of the evening so that you can get used to being with him without having to talk. Then afterward you already have a perfect shared experience to discuss—the movie! Believe it or not, if you employ these tactics and work hard to hide your nervousness, it will eventually come naturally to you and you'll realize that you're not acting anymore. It worked for me; hopefully it will work for you.

Do you have questions about love? Write to:
Jenny Burgess or Jake Korman
c/o Daniel Weiss Associates
33 West 17th Street
New York, NY 10011

Don't miss any of the books in *Love Stories*
—the romantic series from Bantam Books!

SUPER EDITIONS

Coming soon:

RULES & REGULATIONS FOR THE

★NSYNC ®

LIMITED EDITION CD & POSTER GIVEAWAY

I. HOW TO ENTER

NO PURCHASE NECESSARY. Enter by printing your name, address, phone number, and date of birth on a 3" x 5" index card and mail to: Love Stories *NSYNC* CD Offer, BFYR Marketing Department, Bantam Doubleday Dell Publishing Group, 1540 Broadway, 20th floor, New York, NY 10036. Entries must be postmarked no later than October 15, 1998. LIMIT ONE ENTRY PER PERSON.

II. ELIGIBILITY

Sweepstakes is open to residents of the United States and Canada, excluding the province of Quebec. The winner, if Canadian, will be required to answer correctly a time-limited arithmetic skill question in order to receive the prize. All federal, state, and local regulations apply. Void wherever prohibited or restricted by law. Employees of Bantam Doubleday Dell Publishing Group, Inc.; its parent, subsidiaries and affiliates; and their immediate families and persons living in their household are not eligible to enter this sweepstakes. Bantam Doubleday Dell is not responsible for lost, stolen, illegible, incomplete, postage-due, or misdirected entries.

III. PRIZES

Forty (40) Grand Prizes: each consists of an *NSYNC* heart-shaped limited edition CD and signed locker poster (approximate retail value $100.00).

IV. WINNERS

Winners will be chosen in a random drawing on or about October 30, 1998, from all eligible entries received within the entry deadline. Odds of winning depend on the number of eligible entries received. Winners will be notified by mail on or about November 15, 1998. No prize substitutions are allowed. Taxes, if any, are the winner's sole responsibility. BDD RESERVES THE RIGHT TO SUBSTITUTE PRIZES OF EQUAL VALUE IF PRIZES, AS STATED ABOVE, BECOME UNAVAILABLE. Winners will be required to execute and return, within 14 days of notification, affidavits of eligibility and release. A noncompliance within that time period or the return of any notification as undeliverable will result in disqualification and the selection of an alternate winner. In the event of any other noncompliance with rules and conditions, prize may be awarded to an alternate winner.

V. RESERVATIONS

Entering the sweepstakes constitutes consent for the use of the winner's name, likeness, and biographical data for publicity and promotional purposes on behalf of BDD with no additional compensation or further permission (except where prohibited by law). Other entry names will NOT be used for subsequent mail solicitation. For the names of the winners, available after November 15, 1998, please send a stamped, self-addressed envelope to: BDD BFYR, Love Stories *NSYNC* CD Winners, 1540 Broadway, 20th Fl., New York, NY 10036.

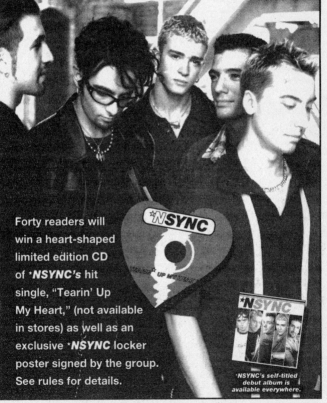